Mia,

Welcome to the Club.
Great to meet you.

Kacey Hammell.

Evernight Publishing

www.evernightpublishing.com

CLUB SPLENDOR: VOLUME ONE

DEDICATION

To the real-life Andy…thank you for sharing your story with me. Your friendship means more than you know.

And for all those who have loved and lost, and then picked yourselves up again, this is for you too.

AUTHOR'S NOTE

Though the settings of Ottawa, Wolfe Island and Gananoque are actual places in Ontario, Canada, some businesses' names and locales have been constructed or modified imaginatively within this fictitious story. Any allowances and/or mistakes are my own.

CLUB SPLENDOR: VOLUME ONE

SWEETEST SALVATION

Kacey Hammell

Copyright © 2013

Chapter One

Andy Sheaver walked through Club Splendor, head down and uncertain as to why she was there exactly. When the thought entered her mind earlier in the week, she'd immediately dismissed it. But the more she pondered it, the harder it was to resist.

She'd never been at the club on her own. Patrick had always made their plans and accompanied her.

Patrick.

Her stomach clenched just thinking about him. She missed him so much.

The decision to come here was not easy. But she thought she'd also feel closer to him just being there. She held that hope close, desperate for a connection to something they shared.

She lifted her head as she drew closer to the maître d. He gave her a bright smile, as well as a look of pity. She'd come to expect it from a lot of people these days.

"Mrs. Sheaver," he grinned and looked down at the black leather appointment book in his hands. "It's wonderful to see you. I hope you've been well?"

She smiled and nodded. "Thank you, Zander. It is good to see you, too."

He looked at her and frowned. "I don't have you on the books for tonight. Perhaps you called and spoke to one of the day staff?"

Uncertain of what the normal protocol was, she'd hoped to get into the club based on past visits. "I'm sorry. I didn't think to call ahead. Patrick always…" Andy trailed off, unable to finish.

Zander gently smiled. Again, the pity in his eyes was not what she wanted to see. But to get in tonight, before she lost her nerve, she would face it.

"Yes, you're right." He looked around, and she could see his mind working. "Why don't you go on ahead and we'll keep this to ourselves. Please do contact me personally anytime." He drew a card from his book and handed it to her. "I'll make sure you're taken care of in the future."

"Thank you so much. I really need to be here tonight." She slid his business card into the small pocket of her black miniskirt.

His hand brushed her shoulder softly. "I understand. Go right on ahead. I'll contact Bridget and let her know you're here. If you'll head to the bar, she'll meet you there."

"Thank you again. If I could request one more favor?" she asked, biting her lip. She hated to ask anything more of his kindness.

"If I can," he checked his watch then gave her his full attention.

"I'd really like to keep my presence here tonight quiet. I'm not sure what room I'll visit and would just like privacy."

Zander's brows drew together. "But Mr. Sullivan will want to know you're here. He always made a point of greeting you and your hus-husband."

"No," Andy ordered. "I don't want Mr. Sullivan to know I'm here. Is he on the premises now?"

The last thing she needed was to see Hunter. Patrick's best friend and owner of the club, Hunter made a point of checking in on her daily. Leaving messages on her machine, texts, and even resorted to calling her in-laws to see if she was all right when she refused to contact him. He was driving her crazy.

She ran a hell of a risk bumping into him here, but she desperately needed to do this. To be somewhere she and Patrick loved to enjoy, and where they'd found so much pleasure. Her first time without him by her side was something she had to find the fortitude to get through.

"All right." Zander interrupted her thoughts. "I'll inform Bridget that you wish privacy and make sure the rest of the staff is aware. Are you sure you're okay?"

Andy met his gaze and hoped her smile was enough to appease him. She wasn't sure of anything, except the need to get out of her house and find someone to take some of the agony away.

"I'm fine. Thank you again, Zander." She pulled out a couple twenty-dollar bills from her pocket and held them to him.

"Oh no." He shook his head adamantly. "I couldn't. Please, just enjoy and please come find me should you need anything."

"Nonsense." She grabbed his hand and pushed the bills into it. With one last smile, she left his station and walked down the dim hallway toward the bar.

Club Splendor always stole her breath. Soft and warm jazz filled the air, and her heart thudded. Patrick had introduced her to the genre of music when they were dating and it was something she adored making love to. She drew in a deep breath and looked around the room as she leaned on the bar.

Nearly eleven months since she'd last been there. The room still had that warmth to it, but the colors of gold and black had been replaced with silver and red. In the far corners of her mind, she recalled Hunter talking about remodeling some of the rooms to keep things fresh and exciting for the patrons.

She had to admit his choices were sensual and inviting. She'd always admired his business savvy and taste in the finer things. So different from Patrick, who always had a difficult time just matching his tie and dress shirt. Their friendship was something she'd always wondered about. They were so different, it was almost like opposites attracting. But their bond was unbreakable.

A light touch on her shoulder made her jump.

"I'm sorry, Mrs. Sheaver. I didn't mean to startle you." Bridget, the club's hostess, smiled at her.

Andy jerked in surprise when Bridget's arms came around her in a light hug.

Throat tight, she patted Bridget on the back. The young woman always had a soft spot for Patrick but never felt an ounce of jealousy whenever he would flirt with Bridget. She often found it sweet and delicious that someone would have an innocent crush on her husband. Patrick was a man who liked to flirt but would never stray.

She pulled back and smiled for the first time in a long while. "Thank you." She caught the tears forming in the other woman's eyes and clenched her hands tight. "Here now, it's all right."

A lump formed in Andy's throat and her body trembled with sorrow. She couldn't allow tears to fall, or it would take forever to stop them again. "Could you get me a glass of white wine, please?"

It was best to keep Bridget focused so she wouldn't shed any tears of her own. That she'd cared so much about Patrick was kind, but she wasn't here for condolences.

Bridget breathed in deep and nodded. "Of course. Any room in particular you'd like to be taken to?" She turned and waved the bartender closer. "A white wine, please, David. No tab."

"I can't allow you to do that. David, please make sure you put that on our—my usual tab. Sheaver." She narrowed her gaze at him, brooking no arguments.

"Yes, ma'am," David replied and set about pouring her drink.

"Mrs. Sheaver," Bridget began.

"Andrea or Andy. I hear Mrs. and have to look around for my mother-in-law," Andy reminded her. "And Patrick would give you a good slap on the ass if he were here."

Bridget smiled gently and blushed. "Yes, you're right. Andy, I…"

"It's okay, go ahead. What is it?"

"I'm surprised to see you here. I'm glad you are, but nonetheless, I am surprised." Bridget handed her the glass of wine that David passed to her.

Andy accepted it, and took a small sip. The liquid was cool and gentle as it slid down her parched throat. "Yes, I imagine a lot of people would be surprised to see me. But I needed to get out of the house. To be somewhere Patrick and I enjoyed together."

Eyes sad, Bridget stepped closer and wrapped an arm around Andy's waist. "I miss seeing him. He was the most special man."

Andy didn't understand why she felt so drawn to this woman. Perhaps it was their shared appreciation and love for Patrick. Or maybe she simply understood and didn't push Andy to share feelings or try to take care of her.

She slid her arm around Bridget's slim waist and gave her a gentle squeeze. "Thank you. I know he enjoyed your company whenever we were here. You and he shared great many jokes and laughter. He adored you."

Bridget sniffled and stepped back when her phone rang. Over Bridget's shoulder, Andy saw Hunter's name come up on the screen and moved back a few feet. "Duty calls. Go ahead. I'm just going to wander."

"I won't let him know you're here, Andy. Zander texted me about your wish for privacy." She pushed a button on her phone and spoke into it. "Mr. Sullivan, how are you this evening?"

With a final wave at Bridget, Andy turned and followed another hallway farther into the club.

Erotic pictures of men and women locked in embraces, women pleasuring other women and groups of people finding ecstasy in one another's arms lined the walls. Andy remembered the first time she'd walked this area.

Arm in arm with Patrick, her cheeks flushed in embarrassment, she'd averted her gaze repeatedly. Only to shift back often when curiosity got the better of her. Patrick always kissed her heated cheeks and chuckled. He'd wanted to show her all the pleasures of the flesh that he could.

Theirs had been an honest and trusting marriage full of hot nights, erotic weekend trips and lovemaking that continued to haunt her dreams. He'd shown her in more ways than she could count just how much he loved her. Every day had been something new, some sexy and erotic text or letter on the pillow beside her when he'd left for work.

They hadn't needed Club Splendor to spice up their marriage. Some nights she'd been so exhausted from the multiple orgasms he'd give her that she'd felt drunk afterward. When he'd first told her about the club, she'd balked and said absolutely not. But the more he'd told her about the pleasures people found there, the more her curiosity and imagination ran rampant. Within a month, they'd made their first trip to the club and had become members a week later.

She found the titillating and exciting sex within the club's walls added a higher level of electricity and stimulation to their sex life. From threesomes to D/s relationships to females pleasuring one another…acts she quickly realized that she loved to watch. She'd never thought of herself as a voyeur before, but couldn't leave the club any evening without witnessing something. Most nights she and Patrick had made use of one of the rooms, the toys there and the exhilaration of being watched as well.

The club was exclusive and Hunter was firm about who were given the right of passage to walk the halls and interact with other members. He screened every couple carefully. Safety for everyone was his main priority.

Her teeth clenched thinking of Hunter.

She couldn't face him tonight. Oh he'd be livid when he learned she was there. She and Patrick had never entered the club without the other present. It had been a silent agreement they had and no other members had approached them to join in their fantasies separately.

Many members often requested their interaction with them, but she and Patrick had chosen not to enter such situations. They would rather look and not touch. Within months, others had stopped approaching them. Patrick had told her once that Hunter had made it known that they didn't wish to interact with anyone else so they'd stopped asking.

Hunter had also made it known that he would take care of cancelling her membership to the club after Patrick's death. At the time, she hadn't thought anything of it and didn't comment. But this past week, as she'd thought of returning to the club and the need to do so overwhelming her, anger over the fact that he'd have the audacity to make such a decision for her was all-consuming. Who the hell was he to interfere in her life?

It was her life, not his. Her plan. How far she was willing to go tonight was unlike anything she'd done before.

She needed to absorb the memories of happier time with her husband. Except her recent thoughts were darker, more punishing than anything she'd ever considered pushing herself into. The Images running through her mind were so different and beyond what she'd shared with Patrick. Oddly enough, they made some of her agony more bearable.

Andy didn't understand the driving need to take part in activities that she hadn't before, but felt dangerously close to the edge. Sometimes she wished she had the courage to end the misery herself, but never could.

She had no idea what else to do.

Stopping in front of Room Six, Andy took a deep breath. Hunter had been gracious enough to give her and Patrick an exclusive room to use. A perk of Patrick's friendship with him, she supposed.

She'd always liked the extra privacy having a room to themselves allowed. And she loved it even more that windows lined one wall of the room, affording her the ability to watch other couples or groups having sex.

Hand on the doorknob, she closed her eyes and turned it. Walking into the room, her breath hitched. Tears filled her eyes.

Just seeing the familiar surroundings, she wanted to flee. The soft, black leather sofa and matching loveseat where she and Patrick had made love countless times called to her. She closed the door and walked over to the sofa. She sat and ran her hands over the material. Cool to the touch. She shivered.

She set her now empty glass on the side table and leaned back. The comfort of the sofa felt good against her back and the air conditioning cooled her heated skin. Smiling gently, relaxation set in a little.

For the first time in nearly a year, a sense of calm washed over her. She was glad she'd come here. She missed Patrick terribly, but needed to find some way to release the guilt and loneliness that threatened to consume her.

Andy reached out and picked up the remote on the side table. She pointed it at the wall in front of her and a curtain opened.

Behind the glass, a young couple—if she had to guess they were probably in their late twenties—captured her attention.

A bed sat in the middle of the small room. The room was barely bigger than a bathroom with only a small vanity and commode. But the surroundings weren't what she was really interested in looking at.

Bound, hands tied behind her, a blonde woman stood with legs apart and stared straight ahead. Naked but for nipple clamps, nipples extended, she was a beautiful sight. A man stood to the side of her with a long, black flogger in his hand. Dressed only in blue jockey shorts, his cock stood at full attention.

Andy wet her dry lips.

Dark hair, flat and rippled abs, muscular build, the man was sexy. Powerful. Her pussy quivered.

She closed her eyes. Guilt rushed over her as desire and adrenaline mixed in. There hadn't been with another man since Patrick and she never wanted to be with anyone.

But when she lifted her gaze and watched the man run the flogger over his partner's body, slapping her breasts and pulling the nipple clamps, the desire to join them nearly choked her.

She'd never joined any of the couples before.

There never seemed to be a need to allow anyone else into the sex she and her husband shared.

But now, the need was strong.

With a deep sigh, Andy resolved herself to the inevitable. The same thoughts that had plagued her all week, to do something different, break out of hiding and find a way to make the pain go away, rushed back. Even if only for one night.

Her guilt and pain would never go away, but maybe for a little while she could put it aside to feel something else. Anything that didn't feel nearly as suffocating. She didn't deserve to move beyond her own pain, but needed to find a way to endure it.

Andy stood and moved across the room. With a light knock on the window, she hit another button on the remote in her hand. The man's gaze lifted and stared wide-eyed at her.

All rooms were outfitted with the windows to fulfill their voyeuristic pleasures, but if the patrons wished to participate, they only had to push the "view" button and those on the other side of the glass could see them too. Participation only needed to be requested, and then it would be up to the couple or group to allow another person into their pleasure.

She pushed the "slide" button and the glass parted in the middle. She smiled, appreciating the ingenuity of the club's devices and hidden gems.

The couple stared at her.

She took a deep breath. "Hello," she greeted them with a small smile and set the remote on the table beside the window.

The woman blinked, her blue eyes meeting Andy's.

Andy shifted her feet, unsure what to say to the woman who might not want another female joining in their interlude.

She didn't feel awkward for long when the man reached out his hand. She hesitated just a few seconds, then laid hers in his and climbed the few steps into the room.

"I'm Nolan," he smiled and brushed his thumb over the back of her hand.

Sparks exploded along her arm and she clenched her thighs together as she came to a standstill.

He was a fine-looking man and his presence so close sent shivers down her spine. His hazel eyes swam with desire and kindness. She hadn't been this close to a man in so long. She swallowed, nipples beading beneath her bra. Her hand tightened in his and she smiled back.

"This is my wife, Paige."

"I'm Andy. Sorry to interrupt." She paused. What did she say? That she wanted to fuck him while his wife watched? "Um."

"Don't be shy, Andy, we've been members here a long time. We know the routine."

She looked at Paige, saw the understanding and acceptance in her blue eyes. Andy suddenly realized she'd seen Paige in the club before but had never exchanged words with her. If she wasn't mistaken, Paige had also been at her house when Patrick had...

She couldn't think about that now. That this woman knew about her recent tragedies was too much. The need to leave made her turn her back. "I'm sorry, I shouldn't have interrupted you. Please, let's just forget about it." She headed back down the steps, desperate to get away.

"Wait, Andy. Please." Paige's soft voice compelled her to turn around. Andy stopped on the bottom step and looked up at the other woman.

Paige looked at her husband. "Honey, I'm feeling really tired right now. Are you okay if I just sit and watch you and Andy?"

Her gaze dropped to Andy again, her eyes conveying the approval to take the offer. How anyone who barely knew her could be so generous and understanding confused her.

She didn't deserve anyone's kindness. Not after what she'd done.

"Please, I'm going to leave and let you both enjoy the rest of your evening. Thank you for the offer."

"Andy, you don't have to go," Paige commented. "Come back up and let Nolan take your worries away. Trust me. He's exceptional at making me forget any kind of trouble."

Andy saw the love, respect and devotion in the couple's eyes as they shared gazed at one another.

She missed seeing a look like that staring back at her every day.

Chapter Two

Nolan reached his hand out to her again. "You're a very beautiful woman, Andy. It would be my pleasure to take your cares away for the evening."

Paige moved to the red cushioned chair in the corner and crossed her legs. Andy had to admire her confidence to sit naked like that.

She smiled at Nolan and gave him a small nod.

Andy put her hand in his once more and allowed him to help her up the steps. He pulled her into his arms as she cleared the top. She was caught off-guard when his head swooped low and his mouth claimed hers. She jerked back with a gasp.

Looking up at him, her hands clenching his biceps and her pulse raced.

Could she do this? Have sex with a man who wasn't Patrick?

No, she had to stop thinking about him.

Anxious to feel anything other than guilt and anguish, Andy lifted her arms and circled Nolan's shoulders. She lifted her face and their mouths met.

His lips were gentle and patient as he allowed her to take the lead. Her tongue caressed the brim of his mouth until it opened. His tongue swirled against hers while his hands travelled down her back.

His touch made her skin burn beneath the black silk camisole she wore. Goosebumps spread along her skin and she shivered. Desire and need nearly drowned her. The need to let out the hidden animal clawed at her to be set free.

Andy ran her hands over his shoulders and down his arms. Her fingers moved over his chest and stopped at his nipples. His breath hitched as she pinched and played.

She moaned when her pussy tightened. Her hands slid down his strong abs and into the waistband of his boxers.

Nolan lifted his head and stepped back. "Wait a minute, hon, let's take it slow. Undress for me."

Andy frowned, her body quaking with need. "What?"

Nolan's jaw clenched and his gaze narrowed. "Do as I say. Undress. Now."

She looked over at Paige, who nodded and gave her a smile of encouragement.

Understanding dawned.

Nolan was the Dom to Paige's submissive and he was playing the role he'd been in when she'd interrupted them. Andy hadn't thought much about what to do once she'd joined them, but the idea of submitting to him never crossed her mind.

Resolved to the need coursing through her and desperation to let herself go, she dropped her hands to her side. She grasped the zipper of her skirt, pulled it down, shoved her thumbs into the waistband and pushed the skirt down over her hips.

It pooled at her feet and she stepped out of it. She lifted her left leg to take off her high heels when Nolan commanded, "Leave them on."

She did his bidding, and crossed her arms over her waist, lifted the camisole up and over her head. Her gaze locked on his when she stood before him in a matching purple bra and thong.

She'd always had a fetish for Victoria's Secret lingerie and had drawers full of it. This was the first time she'd worn any of it in months. She gave her head a small shake and took a deep breath. There was no time for any thoughts of the past.

Nolan stepped toward her, ran his fingers over her shoulders. The flogger ends trailed against her skin, made it tingle. Her eyes closed and her head fell back.

Embers of heat ignited along her body as his hands swept over her. Her nipples tightened, her hips shifted. She wanted nothing more than to straddle him, let him fill her.

Drawing in a calming breath, she lifted her eyes. Nolan smiled, his fingers slid over her bra and nipples. They beaded. Ached.

Andy shuddered. Her fingers wiggled at her sides, desperate to touch herself to ease their throbbing. But she wanted Nolan's hands on her instead.

"You love to be touched. And so sensitive. I like that," Nolan remarked and raised the flogger. He feathered it along her arms, over her shoulders and down her chest. The light touch made her fists clench. She understood a D/s relationship enough to know not to move unless directed.

It was not a role she was used to.

No, stay in the moment. Do not think about the past.

"What will your safe word be?" Nolan asked.

"Charity," she said without hesitation.

She moaned as he ran the flogger down her torso, and over the front of her thong. Her pussy tightened and her clit swelled. She needed to feel his fingers between her legs, rubbing her clit. She shivered, aching to have them deep inside her.

A mind-blowing release was all she could think about.

She gasped. Nolan pulled the flogger back and struck her firmly. Her clit pulsed and her knees shook. "Nolan," she growled.

"I did not give you permission to speak," he commanded.

Her gaze locked on his, desire mirrored in his eyes that she knew was in hers.

Over and over, he slapped her with the flogger—against her center, each nipple and along the shoulders. Her body shook with the need to be fucked.

It had been too long. She was desperate. Her mind clicked with images, as if watching a movie, from scene to scene. She imagined Nolan on top of her, behind her, spanking her, filling her with any of the toys that were in the other room.

To feel a man's cock inside her, pounding, relentlessly pushing her against a table, chair, wall…wherever he wanted, as long as it was soon.

"Keep your hands at your side," Nolan directed as he walked around her. The flogger glided over her ass cheek, and her breath caught. Her legs barely kept her upright. She wouldn't be able to hold on much longer. She'd love to find a seat on top of Nolan's cock.

Her gaze landed on Paige in the chair. The other woman's feet were planted on the seat of her chair, knees laid back against the arms, fingers over her own clit and slowly moving in circles. She looked to have no cares in the world and was leisurely waiting for her husband to come out of a grocery store. Her slow movements held Andy's gaze and her own clit pulsed in response.

She could almost feel Paige's fingers circling her own nub, driving her higher and higher into blissfulness. Paige's red, swollen bud stood out against her pale skin. Andy had never thought about being with a woman before, and while she was ready for just about anything tonight, down deep, she wasn't ready for that. But she did enjoy watching Paige pleasure herself while her husband played with her.

A shout erupted from Andy's mouth as the flogger slapped her on the ass. Her gaze locked with Paige's—

shock and uncertainty filled her. She'd never been spanked before.

As the sting subsided, she smiled. It heightened her senses to what her clit and body were feeling directly.

Paige returned the smile and looked at her husband. "She loved that, baby."

"Yes, I think she did. I can see her juices running down her thigh, babe." Nolan replied, pleasure in his tone.

Indeed, her pussy couldn't contain her juices. She was slick and ready to be fucked. But she found the wait made it all more intoxicating. She needed more.

She opened her mouth to speak, but remembered the setting and closed it again.

"You may speak," Nolan stated.

Andy closed her eyes, and said, "Yes, I loved it. More please."

"Bend over, spread your legs wider and grab your ankles," he ordered.

She did as he asked, ass in the air.

Nolan ran his hands over her cheeks, fingers clenching and tight She moaned as he squeezed hard and ran his palms over the globes as if to soothe. His fingers worked their way into the string of her thong and tugged.

She rocked on her heels, gasping when the string broke and the garment dropped to the floor. The cool air on her pussy was exhilarating and her juices flowed. At this rate, there'd be a pool beneath her and she hadn't even been fucked yet.

Andy relished in the feeling of being naked, save for her bra, and a man's hands gliding over her skin.

The flogger came down on her ass again, hard and swift. She clenched her ankles tight in her grasp and absorbed every sting.

"Let me hear her, baby," Paige requested from the corner.

Nolan chuckled. "Naughty wench," he directed at his wife. "You may speak, woman. Let my wife hear you."

Andy's body shook as the flogger slapped against her ass over and over. It wasn't enough.

"More. Harder. I need it hard, please," she begged. She heard the desperation in her voice. She only hoped he could give her everything she needed tonight.

She swung her long, brown hair over to the side and looked to her left. Nolan raised his arm and brought the flogger down again. "Yes! God, yes," she breathed and lifted her ass higher. "More, dammit, more. Please, sir."

Her pleas rang out in the room and her nipples beaded. If she didn't have to hold on to her ankles to stay in position, she would rip the offending bra away and let the air wash over the beaded tips.

But she couldn't move if her life depended on it. Their heavy breathing and loud slaps filled the room. Her juices flowed and her hips moved in time with Nolan's ministrations.

"You love my husband's pleasure, don't you?" Paige's question caught Andy off-guard.

Her gaze locked on the other woman's fingers working faster against her clit. Andy licked her parched lips. "Yes, I love it. I need more."

Paige lifted her fingers, put them in her mouth, then lowered them to her pussy again. Gazes locked, Paige pushed two fingers inside herself and slowly moved them in and out. "Give her more, baby. She wants it hard and fast, I think."

Nolan said nothing, only brought the flogger down harder and more rapid against Andy's ass. She closed her eyes as her hips jerked and lifted higher every time he lowered the small whip.

"God, yes. Mmm, feels so good," Andy groaned, moving closer and closer to the edge of ecstasy.

"Fuck her, Nolan," Paige demanded.

Andy's eyes opened, surprised. She'd thought Nolan was the Dominant. But since joining them, she realized it might just depend on the situation. Nolan whipped her ass a couple more times, then threw the flogger over his shoulder.

He clasped Andy's waist to help her stand. He undid the hook of her bra and let it fall away. His arms came around her and palmed her breasts. Andy moaned as he pinched and rolled her nipples. Her left hand covered his as he pulled. The other cupped the back of his neck as her head turned and lips met his.

Their tongues dueled and plundered. Andy heard Paige moan and one of her own erupted. Nolan's right hand slid down over Andy's stomach and over her folds. His fingers easily found her clit. He relentlessly circled the bud. She widened her stance as her teeth nipped his bottom lip.

Andy pulled back and laid her head against his shoulder while his fingers worked over her. He pinched her nipple with one hand while the other rubbed her clit. She was awash in glorious lust and desire. She shut her mind off to everything but the groans and gasps filling the room.

Closer and closer, Nolan's fingers worked her toward the edge of release. She wanted a cock inside her, but wasn't sure she should voice it. She didn't know what the boundaries were for this couple. She should have asked before now. She could have brought a dildo in the room with her.

A guttural moan rushed out of her and she cried out, "Fuck!"

"Oh, Nolan. She needs to be fucked. I want to watch you fuck her."

Andy nearly wept hearing Paige give her husband permission to give her what she needed.

Nolan groaned and his hands left her. Andy sighed, comforted by the fact that his chest still aligned her back to keep her upright. She heard the rustle of plastic. She hadn't even thought of protection.

The club had a golden and unrelenting rule about condoms. Everyone needed to wear one when they with someone other than their own spouse. Bowls of condoms were all over the club. Even on the bar. She was thankful Nolan had the foresight to see to it.

"I'm going to fuck you so good," Nolan stated.

Andy looked at him over her shoulder. "I hope so." She licked her lips and shifted to the end of the bed. It was the perfect position for Paige to see her husband slide in and out of her, and allowed Andy the opportunity to watch the other woman play with herself.

She slid her palms over the blue satin sheets and bent over until her hips met the mattress edge. Holding herself up by her arms, she waited for Nolan to finish rolling on the condom.

She smiled, not waiting long as he grasped her hips and rubbed his cock against her clit.

Her smile faded as her arms gave out and she bent even farther against the bed, forearms resting flat on the bed. Her pussy clenched in anticipation—eager and needy.

"Look how wet her pussy is, baby. Hmm, I can see her juices from here," Paige said, lust in her tone.

"The juices are thick and warm against my cock. Christ, baby, fucking her is going to be so good."

"Hurry, I want to watch. I need to come, baby. Fuck," Paige groaned low.

Andy looked to her right. Paige pumped her fingers in and out of her wet center. Her own pussy clenched in eagerness for the same thing.

Nolan continued to rub his cock against Andy's pussy. She lowered her right hand to her clit, widened her stance, and circled the swollen nub. Her hips jerked and lifted.

Desire coursed through her. Her nipples tightened. "Rub your clit harder, Paige," Andy ordered, surprised by the demand falling from her lips.

She desperately needed relief, but she couldn't be so greedy as to not give Paige some of the same treatment. Paige allowed her husband to fuck a woman they'd never really met before, after all.

"That's it, honey. Yes, rub that pussy," Nolan ordered Paige. He stroked his cock up and down Andy's slit.

Andy's fingers moved in tandem with Paige as she fondled her own clit. It had never been so swollen or ached in so long. She had left her own needs too long. The need for a hard and fast release fueled her. She could think of little else.

"Fuck, I have to get inside you. Now," Nolan roared as he entered her.

Andy screamed and both hands clenched the bed sheets as he pushed inside her. He settled deep and paused. "You okay?" he questioned.

"Yes, yes, just fuck me, please," Andy growled.

He pulled back, then pushed roughly inside her again. She was tight probably. Her muscles compressed around his cock as they tried to relax enough to let him move in and out. The months with no sex had made her snug.

She widened her stance again and relaxed her hips. Nolan's cock moved in and out of her, the walls of her pussy thrummed and pulsed with each stroke. As he pumped in easier, she closed her eyes and drowned in the sensations.

"Fuck, you look good moving in and out of her, babe," Paige whispered, desire clear in her voice.

Andy couldn't agree more. Though she was unable to see him, it felt like heaven.

She shook herself from her thoughts and pushed some of the amazing pleasure aside. She knew what she needed. What she deserved.

"Harder. Sir, make it hurt," she ordered.

Nolan's hips pumped faster. She moaned deep, still wanting more. He smacked her ass. Her pussy clamped down and pulled his cock in deeper.

He moaned, "Fuck, yes. Christ that's amazing."

Andy looked at him over her shoulder. "More, deeper. Spank me harder. Give me pain."

"Andy," Paige began, hesitation in her voice.

"No. Do it, sir, please," Andy begged.

Months of guilt and agony had overwhelmed her. It was nothing that she didn't deserve, but she needed to feel some of the hurt she'd brought into others' lives. She shouldn't be free of the anguish that she'd caused. And this was the only way she knew how to be punished.

Nolan's hips pistoned against her ass. He pounded her pussy, slapping her cheek as he went deep.

Andy lowered her hand to her clit again. Her fingers swirled the swollen nub and clenched the bed sheet in her other hand.

"Yes, more. Give it harder." The roles of who was Dominant and submissive forgotten. She just needed him to be ruthless with her.

Nolan groaned and grew thicker inside her. The edge drew close and Andy tightened her inner muscles.

"Damn it, I won't last if you keep doing that," Nolan growled.

His cocked pounded in and out of her and their deep gusts of breath filled the air around them. Andy looked at Paige, watched as she pumped her fingers in and out of her pussy. It was beautiful. But she couldn't allow herself to be caught up in Paige. She needed to concentrate on Nolan fucking her.

Her fingers left her clit as she shifted her stance more firmly onto her left leg and lifted her right one onto the bed.

Nolan moved with the change in position, and shouted, "Christ!"

Andy felt him deeper than ever, thankful that it brought him in closer. He clenched her hips tight and pushed his cock in higher and deeper.

"Fuck me, yes. I need it to hurt," Andy begged. Desperation clawed at her as she straightened her back just a bit more.

Hands tight at her waist, Nolan steered her hips as they dropped onto his cock while he pushed higher. She felt as if she sat on top of him, riding him, except not facing him.

His strong hands maneuvered, pulling her hips down as he pushed up.

White light suddenly filled her vision, catching her off-guard. She gasped. "Christ, I'm coming soon. Almost there. Please, more."

Nolan curled over her back, thrusting deeper into her as she came down onto his cock.

"I can't hold back much longer," Nolan moaned.

Andy lowered her right hand to her clit and pinched it. She cried out and rolled her hips faster. The drive to the edge of the cliff approached fast. She wanted to hold back but didn't deserve such pleasure. Not without pain.

She wanted Nolan to spank her, slap her pussy with his fingers, she didn't care. But she needed the pain.

She pinched her clit harder, her pussy tightened on his cock and she shuddered. It took over and she was helpless to stave off the release she so desperately ached for.

"She's close, Paige. Baby, come with us," Nolan cried out to his wife.

"Yes, love. I feel as if you're fucking me. Mmm," Paige moaned.

Andy heard their voices, but slipped into her own world. Patrick and Peter's faces swam in front of her.

She closed her eyes tight, tears filling them. No, she couldn't think of them at a time like this. She deserved no happiness. They had no place here. She just wanted to be fuck, and without emotion.

"Deeper. Faster," Andy commanded.

Nolan let go of her hips and cupped his hands around her shoulders as he pumped harder and faster inside her.

Yes! This was what she wanted.

In the position she was in, she was surprised he didn't snap her in two. Her back arched as her hips rode his. Her right leg ached at its angle, but she didn't care. She had the pain with the pleasure.

Nolan lowered his left hand and grabbed her nipple. He pulled until it distended as far as possible. She cried out as pain washed through her.

Releasing her, he grabbed her right leg, lowered it to the floor and pushed her completely face down over the edge of the bed.

Unable to move, Andy shivered. Her pleasure soared, as if she were held captive.

Nolan's cock pushed into her, hard and fast. The strength of his hips gave her everything she wanted as he thrust deep.

She turned her head to the right. Her gaze connected with Paige's blue eyes and saw nothing but lust and pleasure. Her gaze dropped to Paige's pussy as she fingered herself, the juices visible.

"Fuck, I'm gonna come," Nolan growled.

Andy watched Paige fuck herself as Nolan pumped harder. The rush of pleasure pushed her toward release.

"Spank me," Andy mumbled into the bedding, unsure if Nolan could hear her.

As his palm hit her cheek, she shouted and her fingers clenched tight against the mattress. Her hands curled into fists and she pounded the bed.

"More, dammit. It doesn't hurt enough," Andy demanded vehemently.

Nolan's hips pistoned faster as he hit her ass over and over. She felt him grow in width inside her and moaned.

"Harder. Make my ass red," Andy cried as her release crashed over her.

Nolan's hand came down once more as he thrust deep. He squeezed the skin of her ass so tight Andy's eyes filled with tears. She exploded with a long, guttural shout and stars filled her vision.

At a distance, she heard Paige and Nolan find their simultaneous release. Nolan drove inside her as her muscles squeezed over and over. He let go of her skin and petted her ass cheek.

Andy buried her head in the bedding and fought to keep her tears at bay.

As her pulse slowed and heart rate decreased, Nolan pulled from her body.

Exhaustion clawed at her. Boneless, she lowered herself onto her knees at the end of the bed and laid her head on the mattress. Closing her eyes, she waited for her breathing to slow.

She felt a hand on her shoulder and opened her eyes. Paige, wrapped in a robe, knelt beside her, a wet cloth in her hand. "Here, to clean up," she said softly.

Andy smiled in thanks and took the cloth. She pushed herself up to the edge of the bed and cleaned herself, then threw the cloth into the tiny pedestal sink in another corner. Staff would come in later and deal with the dirty linens. She was grateful for it since she didn't think she could handle doing it right now.

Nolan walked up beside her and laid her clothing on the bed. Seeing that he was fully dressed, Andy had to wonder how long she'd sat on the floor. It must have been for a good few minutes if they had time to clean up and get dressed.

Andy smiled a little at him, and whispered, "Thank you."

She stood on shaky legs and put her clothes on. Once dressed, she straightened on her heels and walked down the stairs. There was no need to make small talk. She'd probably never see them again.

She looked back at Paige.

The other woman smiled gently. "If you ever need anything, Andy, the club has our number."

Uncertain what to say, Andy turned away and grabbed the remote from the table. She pushed the "close" button and the glass slid together. She hit the "curtain" button and the red velvet shut her away in the room by herself.

She dropped the remote onto the couch, and straightened her clothing. Going without underwear was something for her to get used to, especially in such a short skirt, but she was just heading home. Her ass still stung as the skirt rubbed against it with every move she made.

With a last look around the room, Andy smiled gently, thinking about all the other times she'd spent in this room with Patrick. The stings of pain she'd just experienced would have to be enough for her.

She had no plans to return. The notion niggled in the back of her mind that there were other avenues at the club she could explore, and more pain left for her to feel. There was plenty of time to consider her options, she supposed.

With a sigh, she walked to the door, turned the doorknob and pulled. Head down, she exited the room only to hit a hard wall.

She looked up, taken aback.

Her gaze swept up a white t-shirt covering a rock hard wall of muscle clearly defined beneath.

When she met the stormy, angry eyes of Hunter Sullivan, she gasped.

That he'd found out she was there made her nervous and agitated her. She wanted to avoid him at all costs.

His presence brought forth too much—guilt, fear, anger over his demands and orders these last few months.

The sight of him reminded her of the days on the beach with him, Patrick and Peter. The weekends he would drop in unannounced and crowd into their lives.

But he'd been a part of the family then.

Now, she was ashamed to see him. He made her feel unworthy and a reminder of what she'd done. Not that she really needed it.

His jaw clenched and his gaze narrowed on her. She could almost see smoke coming out of his ears and knew he'd reached his limit with her.

For months, she'd avoided him, which no doubt pissed him off even further. But she couldn't look at him. Her shame was enough without seeing accusations in his gaze.

His nostrils flared. She drew in a deep breath.

Desperate to get away from him, she lifted her hands and gave his chest a hard shove.

When he staggered back, she charged down the hallway as fast as she could.

She deserved his anger and hatred. Every horrible opinion he had of her was justified. Hell, she thought the same things about herself.

Andy pushed her way through the front entrance and raised her hand to catch the attention of a cab, desperate to get away.

She couldn't see her own thoughts mirrored in his eyes.

There was no forgiveness for her. Not even from herself.

And especially not from Hunter.

He would never forgive her for killing his best friend and his godson.

Chapter Three

Andy sat on the cushioned seat of the bay window in her bedroom. Pillows surrounded her as she gazed out into the backyard of the two-story home she'd lived in throughout her eight-year marriage.

She and Patrick had looked at dozens of houses before finding this one. The hardwood floors, three bedrooms, office and spacious kitchen had captured their attention immediately. But the backyard had clinched the deal.

They'd spent many hours working in the garden. Though they only lived about fifteen minutes from the city, they'd planted vegetables on one side and a fair-sized section of roses on the other. Patrick would bring her a long-stemmed rose every day when they were in bloom, and took some to his mother who lived about ten minutes from them. His secretary at the computer software company where he'd worked had been often thrilled when he'd given her an armful just for putting up with him.

God, she missed him.

And she missed her little boy, his laughter and cries of delight as he learned new things.

Hell, she'd give anything to trip over a dump truck or teddy bear again. To find a towel balled up on the bathroom floor after Patrick showered. The little things that used to drive her crazy were the things she missed the most.

Peter tugging hard on her long hair when she tried to get him dressed in the morning. Patrick's incessant humming, or tapping a pen against the table as he tried to figure out the crossword puzzle in the Sunday paper.

She swallowed back the tears that threatened and leaned her head against the window. Two small blue jays fought for their spot at the bird feeder. She found it calming to sit and watch them come by every morning at seven like clockwork. Since she still battled insomnia at night, it became routine to enjoy a cup of tea and watch them fly around her backyard.

She sighed and closed her eyes.

It had been three days since she'd fled from the club and Hunter.

She could still picture the look in his eyes—anger, frustration and disappointment. He'd never looked at her like that in all the years she'd known him—until Patrick and Peter's deaths.

She pushed aside the memories of those dark days she would never escape from. Zombie-like, uncaring and desperate just to be left alone, she only moved through life without really living.

Opening her eyes, she stood and walked through her bedroom and into the kitchen.

After setting her mug in the sink, she leaned on the counter, head down, and her thoughts on the past.

She was grateful for Patrick's planning for their future when they'd first gotten married. He'd handled most of their finances, and his income alone granted her the option of staying at home.

She helped out the local church, fundraising for donations. She'd joined many of the charity organizations her mother-in-law, Jeanine, was a part of. After learning the ropes in organizing various functions to raise money for hundreds of causes, Andy had found a niche in life she excelled at, and had helped multiple charities raise hundreds of thousands of dollars.

In the last year, she couldn't find it within herself to continue doing so. Her life had been shattered. What could she offer other causes when she had lost so much? Where was God when she needed Him most?

She sighed and turned toward the fridge and opened it. Where the shelves were once filled to the brim with fruit, juice boxes, condiments for Peter's favorite hot dog meal, they were nearly bare now. She grabbed a container of yogurt, closed the door and snatched a clean spoon from the strainer of dried dishes.

She leaned against the counter and contemplated what she'd do today. Most days she vegged on the couch and pretended to watch movies or talk shows, but not even Ellen Degeneres could make her laugh.

As she scooped the last bit of yogurt from the tub, the doorbell rang. Her gaze checked the time on the microwave—eight-fifteen. Only her in-laws stopped by these days, but never at this early hour.

Walking through the kitchen and into the foyer, she caught sight of herself in the mirror beside the coat closet. Her brown tresses were all over her head, and she smoothed them down a bit with her fingers. It was a losing battle. She wasn't expecting anyone and the solicitor or whoever was at her door could just live with her faded grey sweats and bugger off. Visitors should call first. Though it wouldn't have mattered—sweats and t-shirts were all she wore at home now.

She unlocked the door and swung it open.

Andy's stomach pitched and her eyes widened. Hunter stood on her porch, arms spread as he leaned against each side of the doorframe. His unwavering gaze met hers.

She knew at some point that he would confront her after the other night. He'd been none-too-pleased to see her at the club then.

He looked even unhappier now.

Hunter Sullivan took a long look at the woman before him.

For years, he'd seen her dressed in long flowing gowns, dress slacks or pant suits with gorgeous blouses or shirts at charity functions. He was becoming very tired of seeing her in the same faded sweats whenever he happened to see her.

Of course that was before she'd told him to go to hell and rarely answered the door anymore.

"Can I come in?" he asked, even though he wasn't about to take no for an answer.

Seeing her at the club the other night had nearly put him over the edge. He never wanted her to grace the place again. At least not without him present.

He pushed those thoughts from his mind and crossed the threshold as she stepped back and walked away.

Hunter closed the door behind him and followed her into the living room.

Memories choked him.

He still couldn't get used to not seeing the framed family photos on the wall. Absent were all pictures of Patrick and Peter, photos from Andy and Patrick's wedding day. The dozens of photos of Peter as a baby when he'd learned to walk, a picture taken every three months. The last would have been his fourth year photo.

His nose tickled and his throat tightened. That little boy meant so much to him. The godson he would have done anything for.

Hunter coughed and took a seat in the black recliner across from the matching loveseat where Andy sat.

She picked at what he could only guess was imaginary fluff from the arm of the loveseat. She obviously didn't want to look at him. He sighed.

Coming here today would no doubt result in a hell of an argument, but things had festered too long. He needed to resolve whatever anger she felt toward him and convince her to move on. He hated that she'd closed herself off from everything and everyone she loved.

He spoke to Jeanine and Tony Sheaver every day. Patrick's parents had become his own since first meeting them in his senior year of high school. Even when he and Patrick had left for college, they'd always made sure Hunter came to their house on holidays and special occasions.

Having lost his own drug-addicted parents when he was two, and having moved from one foster home to the other his whole life, meeting the Sheaver family was one of the best things to ever happen to him. On his own since he was sixteen, he'd worked two jobs after school in order to stay in a rundown motel on the outskirts of town.

The couple who owned the motel knew he was alone, and for various chores and help when needed, they'd kept quiet about him being underage and never called the authorities.

Within the first six months of being Patrick's friend, he'd tried to convince Hunter to save the money he spent at the motel and move in with him and his folks.

Hunter's pride kept him from accepting, and he managed to save enough money to live off while he tried to save for college. It was a useless effort since tuition cost more than he could make in ten years just working at the car garage and sweeping up after last call at a bar in town.

He'd been shocked, however, when Patrick and Tony showed up at his motel one evening and revealed that his first year of tuition at college had been paid for. He'd been humbled and had succumbed to tears at their generosity. He'd tried to refuse their gift, but Tony had wouldn't allow it. They would help him like that was more than anyone had ever done for him.

He'd worked hard during those four years and finally graduated with a business degree. He'd worked at the bar, having moved from janitor to bartender, and even became the night manager after a couple of years. Though the Sheavers refused to let him pay any of the tuition money back, Hunter had put it into investments for them once he'd learned the ins and outs of business and stocks.

They now lived off the interest of those investments, and Hunter took pride in knowing he'd paid them back somehow and they were taken care of.

Especially with Patrick gone now.

Hunter sighed, which caught Andy's attention. Her eyes met his briefly before lowering to her hands, which were clenched tight in her lap.

"Look, Andy," he began.

"What do you want, Hunter?" Her forest-green-eyed gaze met his. Anger swirled in their depths.

"I'm tired of this. Dammit." He snarled, rising, and crossed to the fireplace. He ran his fingers through his hair and leaned one arm on the mantel. He looked over at her, stomach churning with indigestion and pain. He'd loved Patrick and Peter too. Could she not understand that she wasn't the only one suffering?

"Tired of what? I never asked you here."

"This!" Hunter spread his arms wide. "You. I'm so tired of seeing you locked away in this house, never leaving and pictures gone."

"Go to hell," Andy spat and leapt to her feet. She moved behind the loveseat, obvious fury making her hands shake as she laid them on the back of it. "You don't have any say in how I live. I never asked for your opinion. If you don't like it, get the hell out of my house. And my life!"

Hunter breathed deep, nostrils flaring. He could no more walk away from her than he could from the Sheavers. She was as much a part of his life, and his heart, as they were.

But his love for her went far beyond sisterly.

He pushed that thought away, buried it deep within himself as he'd done for years. She was Patrick's girl, his wife. He always honored that.

"Dammit, I don't want to argue with you, Andy. But you really need to move on. Live life again and leave this house."

"I leave the house. You don't know what I do every day."

"Oh yes, you go out. Like the other night? Why did you go to the club? I thought we agreed you were no longer a member," Hunter demanded, curious about her answer.

"No. *You* decided I was no longer a member. Not me. I never said I wanted that. Who are you to make decisions for me?" Andy retorted, cheeks flushed, hands on her hips.

Hunter had to admit he was finally seeing a glimpse of the fiery, strong woman she'd been until this last year. He liked her eyes ablaze, jaw clenched and fury radiating off her body. He just needed to provoke her enough and challenge her to move beyond these walls and back to the things she loved to do.

"I don't want to make decisions for you." He took a calming breath. "Listen, the club is not the place for you any longer. Without Patrick… There's no need for you to be there anymore."

"Why do you think that?"

"He was the one who wanted to show it to you. He never really thought you'd come to enjoy it as much as you did. Neither of you interacted with others. What can you find there now without him?"

Andy smiled, cold and detached. He hated that smirk.

"Oh, come now. You know what happens in *your* club. Surely, I don't have to spell it out for you."

Goddamn her.

Yes, he knew what she'd done inside the room she'd once used with Patrick. Though he normally didn't interfere in his members' activities unless there was a problem, he did ask Paige and Nolan if Andy had simply watched. He'd been shocked, then livid, to learn a few details of what happened between the three of them.

Andy had always been a devoted wife to Patrick, faithful to the core. To know she'd been an active participant at the club for the first time had suddenly left him empty and alone.

But he couldn't allow his feelings on the matter to distract him from pushing her back into life.

He shrugged. "No. You don't have to spell it out for me. But is that what you truly want and need in your life? Sex with strangers? Do you need to find comfort in people who don't care about you?"

Andy glared at him. "That is none of your business." Her voice rose as she continued. "What I do in my life is for me to decide. I never asked to have you in my life. Don't expect me to want you there now."

His heart clenched. Her words were like a punch to the gut.

Yes, he'd sort of come as a package deal when she'd married Patrick. But the Sheavers were the only family he had. And when Peter was born, oh, he'd played the dutiful uncle to the little boy. Though she'd never voiced her frustration at his being in attendance at nearly all family gatherings or taking up some of Patrick's time once a week for a guys' night out, he'd understood the stone-faced woman who left the words unsaid.

"I always promised Patrick I'd look after you if he couldn't."

"Fuck off, Hunter. Don't give me that." Her hands fisted at her sides. "Look, please just go. I don't need you here. I have things to do."

He wouldn't be so easily dismissed.

"Things to do? Like what, plan your next adventure at the club? I don't think so. Why? Explain to me why you felt the need to go there?"

Arms wide, she yelled, "I wanted to fuck somebody. Is that what you want to hear? That I wanted to have a cock inside me for the first time in almost two years? I wanted to have a man inside, pounding me—brutal and painful. What better place to do that than at the club where I know I'm safe?"

Hunter's heartbeat accelerated. To know she needed someone that close to her was agonizing. It was a barren and desperate act of someone who had nothing to live for. Or didn't think she was worth much.

"Why pain? You couldn't have found satisfaction in that. No pleasure, Andy? You, of all people, found pleasure in that kind of sex? I don't believe for a moment that you're now into rough sex," Hunter said, gruff. His mouth was dry, and confusion made his head hurt. Would he never understand this woman?

Andy crossed her arms over her chest. She looked out the window behind him. Her gaze was unfocused, filled with pain.

"Yes, pain. It's what I deserve, isn't it?" Her gaze captured his. Hunter felt his heart crack at her desolate look. "I killed the two most important people in my life.

In your life. I just want the pain to make me forget for a little while. To put the guilt and loneliness aside for a few moments at least."

Hunter's legs shook as he stared at the woman he loved. He reached out a hand, found the arm of the sofa and stumbled to sit down. "Andy," he breathed. He shut his eyes. He couldn't take the pain in hers and needed to close himself off from it for a moment.

He'd had no idea just how bleak and lonely she'd become. He'd believed her grief alone had kept her from truly living.

He opened his eyes and watched her wipe the tears from her cheeks. "Andy, sit down, please," he requested softly.

She moved around the loveseat and took a seat, curling her knees up to her chin, arms clenched tight around them. He'd never seen her look more fragile.

He took a deep breath and tried to figure out how to get through to her.

"There is no reason for you to go to such lengths because of any guilt you feel. Neither Peter nor Patrick's deaths were your fault. You have to know that."

Andy looked at him, shocked. "Not my fault! Of course they were my fault. I drove the car that killed my son! My husband died of a broken heart because of it. The full blame lies at my feet."

Hunter couldn't stand it: he had to get closer to her. He lowered himself off the sofa and practically leapt on his knees toward the loveseat. He grabbed her ankles and squeezed. "Andy, a drunk driver hit your car. There was nothing you could have done to stop it. You nearly died yourself. "

"I wish I had died instead of my darling little boy. My sweet angel." Andy dropped her forehead onto her knees. Sobs racked her body.

Hunter's eyes filled with tears. Memories of Peter toddling toward him, calling him "Unc Ter". His heart ached missing him.

"Andy, look at me." He waited until she lifted her head. Eyes and nose red, she was still the most beautiful woman in the world to him. "I understand how you're feeling." He raised a hand when she opened her mouth to object. "I do. I wish I could go back in time and change everything. To bring them both back. But I can't, and neither can you."

He cupped her calves and rubbed softly. "You need to find a way out of your despair and move on. It's what Patrick would want."

She shook her head. "Patrick hated me before he died. His grief and hatred for me is what killed him."

"No, sweetheart, listen." He clasped her hands when she shook her head. "Dammit, hear me. You know about the heart disease that ran in the Sheaver family. Patrick's grandfather and a couple other grandparents before him all died from it. I know the doctors explained it to you. Patrick's heart just stopped beating while he slept. It's not your fault."

"But losing Peter put more stress on his heart. If I hadn't lost our baby, Patrick might still be here. I don't care what the doctors say about some hereditary disease." Andy's hands tightened around his. "He died from a broken heart because I killed our little boy."

Hunter could almost feel the pain shooting from her fingertips.

"I want them back, Hunter," she whispered.

"So do I, sweetheart, so do I." He rubbed her fingers gently with his own, their gazes locked.

He could drown in her eyes. Though he'd kept his feelings buried deep so they never showed when he was around her, there were times when he'd let his guard down a little bit. Sometimes he wished she'd look at him as she once looked at Patrick.

He'd watch the two of them together, kissing, touching and sharing looks across the room. At the club, he'd seen them pet one another, raising their arousal and desire before they'd head home and take care of those needs.

But Hunter had never felt jealous of Patrick. He'd been like a brother to him, and he would never harbor any grudges against him for finding happiness. He'd only wished that he could find someone to love besides the lady in front of him and grow old with her. To see the Sheavers, as well as Andy and Patrick love one another allowed Hunter to believe in it.

"The pain and guilt will one day fade. Until then, you have to continue to live your life and push it away."

"I don't deserve not to suffer. After everything—"

"No, dammit," Hunter cut her off, anger surging within him. "You do deserve happiness again. What you do *not* deserve is to let strangers use you in whatever twisted ways you've thought up in your mind. It's inconceivable to think you'd allow yourself to be treated like that."

Andy pulled her hands from his grasp and huffed out a deep breath. "You don't know anything about it. I'll go back to the club whenever I damn well please."

"No, you won't," Hunter said, smug. "All members of the staff have been given explicit instructions. They will be fired if they grant you access of any kind."

Andy gasped and clenched her fists. Hunter had the feeling she wanted to slug him.

"You didn't! It's not Bridget or Zander's fault," she scowled. "Do you hate me so much that you'd take away the only thing that gives me any kind of way to live with everything?"

"Hate you." Hunter frowned. "Whoever said I hated you? God, Andy, I…"

He caught himself before he said too much. Confessions of his love were the last thing she needed. She'd never believe him, anyway.

"Look, maybe we can spend more time together. Talk, do things that will get you out of this house and help you to move on. I can clear my schedules at work for however long I need to. Everything can be handled over the phone."

Andy shook her head. "No. I don't want pity and do not need your constant nagging. If I can't go to your club, I'll find another one that caters to the same things."

Hunter drew back, stood, and glared down at her. "You'd seriously go to another club that doesn't have the same safeguards I employ, and let strangers use you? Fuck you senseless? I won't stand for it."

Andy shot to her feet, eyes narrowing on him. If he wasn't shaking with rage, he'd find it funny that with her five-foot-three frame, she tried to look mean and commanding against his six-foot-one.

"You have no say in the matter. I make my own decisions."

"You don't need men sweating all over you! Putting you in positions you aren't used to and dominating you. Some places don't have the same guidelines and rules mine does. You could seriously find yourself in a lot of pain at the hands of people who don't care for anything other than their own needs."

"That's just fine by me. I want to feel the pain along with the pleasure. The more pain, the better I can stand someone else touching me. If I can't have the family I love back, then I don't need to feel any kind of pleasure beyond getting fucked. And I don't need, nor do I want, the singles scene. There will never be another man in my life like that. Without Patrick, there is no soul mate for me."

Hunter's fists clenched. He couldn't allow another man to touch her. There was no way he could live with it.

"Stay away from any of those clubs, Andy. I mean it."

Her eyes shot fire at him. She shook her head and gave his shoulder a shove. "Knock it off. If you won't let me into your club, it's your problem. Yes, there I feel safe, I know most of the staff and that you'd never allow anyone to get out of hand. But if you stand in my way, then I'll go elsewhere. Simple as that." She sounded smug, certain she had the upper hand.

His body shook with rage. And fear. To think of her at another club with sleazy men who would tie her up or sweat all over her... It made him ill just thinking about it. She could be seriously hurt. Or worse.

An idea formed in his mind. "So all you want is access to my club and anyone who is willing to join you for sex and a bit of pain? Is that all?" Hunter demanded.

He was crazy to even consider such a plan, but he couldn't allow her out there on her own. Christ, she'd end up even more broken than she was now.

"I want a lot of pain and a lot of fucking, yes." She smiled at him, unaware she prodded the beast within him. Damn her for handling her sorrow like this.

"All right. You can have access to the club. I'll inform the staff of the change," Hunter stated, grinning. "No problem, sweetheart."

Andy's eyes widened. "I'm surprised you're agreeing with this. What changed your mind?"

"You did, actually. If this is the only way you'll try to move forward, then I'll help anyway I can." Hunter stepped closer until mere inches separated them.

Andy tried to take a step back, but she was too close to the loveseat and could go no farther.

"Wait a minute, Hunter," she ordered, her gaze narrowed on him, obviously suspicious. "What's the catch?"

"Catch? There's really no catch. It's my club, I say who comes and goes."

"I know you do, but…" Andy shifted her feet. He could see her mind working and felt the tension radiate off her body. She looked like a caged animal standing before him desperate to escape.

"You were pretty determined to keep me out of the club. I find it odd that you agree with my fucking other men so fast."

Hunter wasn't used to Andy speaking in such a manner. Even at the club, she'd always held herself regal and showed her desires when she found something she liked. But he'd never heard her talk so crude and dirty. He had to admit, he quite liked it.

"Oh, I never agreed to you fucking other men, Andy. Not at all."

She frowned. "But I can frequent the club, right?"

"Of course you can." He clasped her hands in his. "But you can't have sex with anyone else."

"You're forbidding me to interact with people?" she demanded, shocked.

"Not at all. I merely said you couldn't fuck other people. You'll just only do so with whomever I choose."

"You're going to choose whom I have sex with! I don't think so, buster." Andy tried to shift away, but he held fast.

"Yes, sweetheart, *I* will choose. But it's an easy decision for me, so don't worry."

She stopped struggling. Her gaze roamed his face, looking for what he wasn't sure. "I still don't understand."

"It's simple really," he replied, satisfied with his plan. "You can use the club. You're welcome to sit and watch whatever people you wish, but you cannot fuck anyone."

She gasped and her cheeks flushed. "No one? Look, Hunt—"

"No one," He lifted his left hand and tapped the edge of her nose with his index finger. "But me."

Andy fell back against the back of the loveseat, shock written all over her face.

Satisfaction filled Hunter that he'd left her speechless.

He'd meant what he'd said. There would be no other man but him that she'd have sex with at the club. He'd fuck her any way she wanted, anytime she wanted. Hell, he'd even go as far as giving her some of the pain she so desperately claimed to need.

And in doing so, he'd bide his time. Wait as long as it took for her to realize that the sex and pain she was looking for was the opposite of who she was. With all that pleasure and pain, he'd show her that life was worth living and they could be good together.

He'd loved her for over a decade now. A little while longer wouldn't be too hard.

Hunter was nothing if not a patient man.

Chapter Four

Andy entered the club the next evening promptly at nine o'clock. To even be there was surprising to her.

Hunter had left her reeling and confused yesterday. His orders had been simple. Meet him at the club tonight at nine and they'd tackle their first adventure together.

After sitting on the loveseat for what seemed like an eternity, thinking about what he'd said, she'd laughed it away and tried to push it from her thoughts. She'd barely slept all night from tossing and turning. When she had dozed, it was only to have dreams of Hunter's hands on her.

She woke up four or five times, sweating and aching. At five a.m., she'd given up, lay in bed and watched the dark sky turn blue through the window. Guilt ate away at her.

To have such thoughts about her husband's best friend tore her to pieces. She cursed him at every moment in her mind for putting such thoughts there. He'd known she was lonely and without a man for too long. That Hunter would callously make light of how she felt pissed her off.

When she'd finally stumbled out of bed to shower at nine that morning, her fury with him had subsided, but the thought of having sex with him still swirled through her mind.

Just when she'd gotten herself under control and moving around the house enough to clean, his text arrived mid-afternoon.

C u 2nite @ 9. Rm 14. Look fwd 2 c'ing u. H.

She'd dropped her phone on the counter and stepped away as if it were a live snake about to strike. When her heart rate slowed and her hands weren't shaking as much, she'd texted him back.

Don't do this. 4get it. Not what I had in mind.

Her phone had vibrated within seconds. *I'll inform staff u r not a member then.*

Andy had gasped, furious with his strong-arm tactics. Two could play his game. *I'll find 'nother club. I'm sure there's 1 close by.*

It hadn't taken long for his reaction. *Andy. Meet me here. 9. Don't make me look 4 u.*

She'd glared at the phone for about ten minutes, then finally replied, *Fine, but only 2 talk.*

The rest of the afternoon, she'd made quick work of chores she'd put off for too long. Even though her house wasn't a pigsty, she still only cleaned from top to bottom about once every three months in the last year. Making things look neat and tidy for just her alone seemed like a waste.

As she'd gone through the motions, she'd tried not to think of Hunter and what he offered her. There was no way she'd be comfortable having sex with him…no matter how much her subconscious seemed to think so. She'd never thought of him in that way.

Actually, if she were honest with herself, she had. When she'd first met Patrick at Carleton University, they'd become instant friends. He was handsome and sweet, she'd been able to talk to him about anything. But it was Hunter who'd originally caught her eye.

Even back then, he was strong, proud and sure of himself. A lot of women on campus had their eye on him. But he'd seemed more focused on his job and business degree than dating. Though they'd spoken a few times whenever the three of them were together, she'd found she'd had very little in common with Hunter.

When Patrick asked her out the first time, she'd been surprised but pleased. Their first kiss had made her toes curl, and they were inseparable every day after that.

Her once minor attraction for Hunter never crossed her mind.

Until now.

Suddenly, it was like a never-ending loop in her head.

She caught sight of Zander behind his small desk and smiled. When she approached, he waved her on.

"Mr. Sullivan is waiting for you. He said you'd know where to go." He smiled and winked.

Cheeks on fire, she gave him a small nod and walked ahead. She moved into the bar area and looked around. The place was packed tonight.

There were a few people she recognized, but most were new faces. Hunter's business was certainly thriving.

Bridget caught sight of her and waved. Andy did the same and turned to the left, down the hall that would take her to room fourteen and Hunter.

Movement caught the corner of her eye, and she looked to her right. At a table in the far corner, Paige and Nolan sat with another couple. She missed a step, but gained her balance again. She hadn't thought about seeing them again. Paige waved and her husband smiled bright.

The couple's kindness and understanding arced across the room. Andy smiled and waved back. They'd been there for her the other night. She'd be forever grateful for it.

Reaching the room, she took a deep breath and knocked. Hearing Hunter's gruff, "Come in," she turned the knob.

The room, similar to the one she'd used the other night, had a warmer feel to it. The fireplace ablaze, the heat of it welcomed her.

Andy's gaze swept the room. Furnished with a full living room set, she loved the royal purple and black colors of the furniture and curtains than anything else. This room conveyed privacy and self-indulgence. Her heart rate increased just thinking of all that might have been done in this room.

It was made for sex. Especially with a glass display case that took up the most of wall. Inside were dildos, anal plugs, collars, floggers, cock rings and more toys of pleasure.

Andy's gaze landed on Hunter where he sat in the center of the couch, arms stretched over the back of it.

"Hi, sweetheart."

Her gaze narrowed on his and she shut the door behind her. "Don't you sweetheart me, Hunter. And get that look off your face."

"What look?"

"That smug look. I might be here, but not for the reasons you think."

"Then why are you here?" he questioned, his gaze unwavering.

"I wanted to tell you in person that your idea isn't going to happen. We've been... friends too long. You're Patrick's best friend. It's all kinds of wrong."

He leaned forward, arms resting on his powerful thighs.

His red t-shirt molded his shoulders and the cuffs of the arms looked snug around his biceps. Damn him for being in such great shape.

She shivered, nipples tightening. She needed to get away from him.

"There, I've said all I have to say. Goodbye," she muttered, then turned back toward the door.

Hunter was quickly behind her, arms encasing her as his palms pressed against the door and preventing her retreat.

His breath was warm against her ear. Andy wished she'd left her hair down. At least then she wouldn't be able to feel his breath on her neck.

A shudder ran through her. "Let me out, Hunter. I need to leave."

"Why? You were so desperate to remain a member and be here the other night. I'm simply offering a safer solution. Me instead of strangers," he rasped against her ear.

"I don't have to worry about much with strangers. At least they aren't people I have to see after the sex is over."

Hunter pressed in closer behind her, which pushed her farther against the door. She'd always been claustrophobic. And right now, being caged in by this man, made it even harder to breathe than if she was locked in a closet. His chest was firm against her, his mouth against her ear, and his hoarse voice soft.

Her thighs rubbed together and her clit chafed against her thong. The string along her ass was snug. All she had to do was turn around and take what he offered. She wanted a cock inside her.

Dear lord, this was Hunter.

Could she step over the invisible line and take what he offered?

He was attractive, always had been to her. Hell, she'd only been married, not dead. She appreciated a gorgeous man when she saw him.

Hunter always treated with her respect and friendship. She didn't know how much he dated but had heard women at the club mention his prowess in the bedroom. He could probably give her everything she needed. There would be a sense of safety with him at least.

And her body's reaction to him today, while surprising, knew what it wanted. While she was sure it was a bad idea for them to journey down this path, she was overwhelmed by the sudden realization that not just any cock would do.

She wanted Hunter. Wanted only him inside her.

Her breath hitched and her lungs filled, making it hard to breathe. No, she didn`t have the courage to give into this man.

She needed to get out of this room and away from him. Grabbing the doorknob once more, Andy yanked.

Hunter's palms never moved from the door, but in her hasty movements, his chest aligned tighter against her back.

Pressed against the door, she turned her head, her right cheek resting on it as her breasts pushed against her bra. The hard surface scraped against her clothing, which abraded her nipples. The urge to purr and rub against the wood was overwhelming.

Hunter's body pressed against her; the cock cradling her ass told her that he was just as affected as she. His length was hard, solid. His hips dipped and shoved against the crack of her ass.

"Andy," he whispered in her ear.

She closed her eyes, willed herself to push back against him until he let her go.

Her eyes opened when she realized her hips moved against his. Her pussy quivered and her stomach clenched. There was no sense in fighting a losing battle. She wanted him. If it took having sex with him to snap them both out of this odd funk they seemed to be in, then so be it.

Her left arm lifted, curled around his neck and pulled him closer. Her head fell back onto his right shoulder as his arms folded around her and he palmed her breasts.

"Jesus, you feel good," Hunter groaned against her neck.

She closed her eyes and she pushed her ass against his hard shaft while his fingers made quick work of the buttons holding her tangerine silk blouse together. She lowered her arm as he dragged the collar of her shirt down her shoulders. His palmed her breasts again, leaving her arms stuck in the loose sleeves, which made it nearly impossible to move.

He nipped her shoulder with his teeth. She gasped as he undid the front clasp of her bra. Her breasts fell into his hands, and he twisted the nipples between his fingers and thumbs.

Her hips jerked against his, legs shaking. "Hunter," she groaned, arms flexing. She wanted to touch him, but her movements were hindered.

"Christ, your tits are perfect," he growled and flexed his hips against her ass. His fingers played with her breasts. Electricity sparked against her nipples as never before.

Andy looked down. Hunter's hands were flat as only the palms circled her nipples. They beaded and tightened. Shots of heat rushed straight to her pussy.

If not for Hunter pressing tighter against her, she would have fallen on her ass. Her pussy throbbed, aching to be filled. She'd never had an orgasm from just having her nipples played with, but she felt the precipice just on the horizon.

Not wanting to finish too soon, she was able to lower her hands, wrenched the shirt off, and pushed back into Hunter.

"Oh yes, Andy." His teeth nipped her neck hard, then licked it to soothe the sting. "Your ass is so good against my dick."

"Mmm," Andy moaned and placed a hand behind her. She shifted her ass a tiny bit and ran her fingers along his rigid length. "You're so hard."

Hunter's hands squeezed her breasts tight. His hips moved in perfect rhythm with her hand.

He clasped her waist and turned her. Andy looked into his cloudy-grey eyes as she undid the button and zipper of his slacks. Once undone, she slid her hand inside the waistband and found his naked flesh.

Hunter leaned forward to kiss her, but she arched her neck, her head pressing hard against the door. His lips found her neck once again, lavishing her with kisses and nips.

To touch him like this was surreal. She wanted to stroke and pet him, and have him do the same in return. But in the end, she still had to walk away without getting too intimate.

To have him kiss her would make it all too personal. If she could refrain from doing that, no matter how much she longed to taste him, then she might leave the room unscathed.

Andy stroked his cock up and down and spread the pre-cum over his length. He was wide and long, probably bigger than she'd ever had inside her before.

No.

No, she couldn't compare him to anyone else. Especially…

Dammit.

Pulling her hand from his pants, she moaned as his teeth found her nipple. He bit down on her hard. She gasped, back arching, and pushed it farther into his mouth.

Hands at his waist, she applied pressure to walk backward toward the sofa. His head lifted and his gaze met hers. He cupped her cheeks and angled his head low.

She pulled back a bit and smiled at him, putting on a brave face. His lips were a temptation she had a hard time battling.

Andy tucked her fingers back into his pants, and pushed them off his hips. Her hand circled his cock again and pumped him.

"Sweetheart," he groaned, eyes heavy with desire and heat.

"Shh," Andy whispered. She gave him a gentle shove to sit on the center of the sofa and removed his shoes and clothing.

Dressed only in a red t-shirt, his cock standing at full attention, he made Andy's mouth water. She averted her gaze and tried to resist the intimacy of taking him in her mouth. They'd agreed to have sex. That was all she intended to do.

She caught sight of the remote on the table beside the couch. With a grin directed at Hunter, she said, "Let's see what we have behind the curtain."

He reached out a hand. "No, Andy, let it just be the two of us…"

"Shh, let's just take a peek."

The black curtain opened to reveal a brunette sandwiched between two large and well-built men. One lay back on the bed, his cock inside her as she straddled him. The other had his cock shoved inside her ass, and they both fucked her.

Andy had the full view of their asses, could see the two cocks and watched the woman's hips move. She looked down at the remote in her hand and hit the "up" button. Moans and sighs filled the room she and Hunter were in. She lowered the volume a couple octaves so it wasn't so loud, her gaze riveted to the scene before her.

Though she would never want to be with two men, threesomes always fascinated her. To have four hands touch her wherever she needed them was a seductive temptation. It simply wasn't for her. But damn, it was erotic as hell to watch.

She looked back at Hunter, surprised to find his gaze on her rather than the scene in the adjoining room. She winked and undid the button of her slacks. Her fingers slid inside the waistband and turned as she pushed them down her hips to give Hunter a full view of her ass and barely covered pussy. Clad only in a blue thong, her ass high, she made slow work of pulling the slacks over her feet and heels.

His guttural moan spurred her on and she wiggled. She ran her hands along the inside of her thighs, stopping just before her fingers touched her covered sex. She was about to turn and face him when his hands clasped her waist and yanked her onto his lap.

Back to his chest, his cock wedged against her damp thong, Andy leaned back. Her head dropped onto his shoulder. She moaned as his fingers found her nipples and his tongue lapped her ear.

"Look at them, Andy," Hunter directed. "Look at how much she loves those cocks."

Her gaze locked on the trio through the window. The woman's moans, just the sounds alone, went straight to her pussy. It was naughty and almost depraved to be so turned-on by another person's gasps and sighs of pleasure, but Andy felt every noise throughout her body.

She wiggled her feet out of her shoes, lifted her legs onto the edge of the sofa and used her feet to help her rub against Hunter's cock.

His hand slid from her breast, down her stomach and between her legs. He gently rubbed her flesh through the lace thong, and her hips rose to meet each movement eagerly.

Her head angled so he could only reach her neck. She shivered as his teeth scraped the skin. Hunter continued to nibble on the skin as her hips moved against his fingers. Moisture seeped through the lace. The wetness on his fingers made it easier for the material to rub her clit.

"Would you ever let two men fuck you, Andy?"

The question took her by surprise. Her hips slowed, his fingers stopped the torturous pleasure on her clit.

She swallowed. "No. I love to watch, but I don't think I could ever share myself like that."

Hunter's fingers resumed their ministrations and slipped around the lace. He pulled hard and tore the thong from her body. She gasped and her legs fell back, widening further.

She watched Hunter lift the scrap of material to his face and breathed in her scent. His cock hit against her clit, and Andy jerked. The pleasure on his face was wonderful. She'd never seen him look that way before. That he found her essence so pleasurable filled her with confidence and sexual empowerment.

Calm down. Remember, keep it just sex.

Andy's gaze shifted back to the trio on the other side of the window. She grasped Hunter's cock and pressed it against her clit. Her hips canted against it, moisture flooding her channel, and she arched her back.

Hunter's fingers tangled with hers as he pulled his cock away. "I can't reach the condoms, sweetheart."

Andy pinched her nipples, eliciting a moan from him. She sat up and looked over her shoulder.

His gaze captured hers, desire and the honesty he'd always shown her over the years shining bright.

Andy reached forward and picked up a silver packet out of a bowl on the table.

His hand slid down her back, rubbed her spine up and down. "I'm clean too. If you don't want one, we don't need it. Unless…"

She shook her head, and whispered, "I'm still on the pill because of woman issues. But you know there are no guarantees. It's best to be safe."

She tore open the package, put one foot on the floor and lifted her hips from his lap. She gasped when his fingers slid into her pussy as she rolled the condom over his length.

"Fuck, you're so wet," Hunter growled, lust making his voice harsh.

Andy rode his fingers up and down, hips dropping hard. It wasn't enough. His cock looked much wider and longer. He'd go as deep as she needed, she was sure of it.

She lifted off his fingers and resumed her reclining position against him, chest to back, and planted her feet on the edge of the sofa. With Hunter's hands at her waist to help, she lifted and put his cock against her.

Hunter moaned in her ear, face buried in the curve of her neck.

Her gaze locked on the trio in front of her. The woman was on her knees, sucking both cocks, alternating between each one.

Hunter's cock slid inside her, stretching the walls of her channel. Once buried deep, neither moved. His breath was hot against her neck, fingers pinching her nipples gently.

Andy closed her eyes and absorbed the feel of him inside her. Full, tight, burrowed deep, she didn't know where he ended and she began.

"Andy, love," he whispered.

Andy's eyes opened wide and her heart pitched. No, that word had no value here. She cleared her thoughts and lifted her hips.

His cock eased in and out of her. She used his chest behind her as a brace and moved her hips.

"Christ," Hunter moaned behind her, but she didn't want to hear his voice.

She sat up and grabbed her knees. Using them for leverage, her hips rose and fell, seating him deep inside her each time she came down.

Yes, perfect! He hit her in exactly the right spot, going so deep, the pinch of pain was there.

"Andy, slow down," Hunter demanded.

His hands came around her waist as if to slow her, but she put her own over his wrists to hold him in position.

"Fuck me, Hunter,"

"Dammit, shit. I can't resist you."

Andy laughed, free in the swells of rapture that coursed through her. She rode his cock strong and steady; her pussy wept. Her juices made it even easier for him to hit the mark without any resistance.

Her hips jerked. An orgasm was just out of reach.

His hands tightened on her. "Your pussy feels so good around my cock. I'll never get enough."

Her gaze locked on the two men through the window. Cum spilled from their cocks as the woman between them tried to catch it all in her mouth.

Andy shouted in rapture as she rode Hunter's cock. The swift pace pushed her closer and closer to the edge.

As his hands at her waist helped her to move in perfect rhythm, Andy lowered hers and grabbed her breasts. She pinched and pulled her nipples, feeling the pleasurable sting wash over her. She shivered and gasped.

"I've got to cum, sweetheart," Hunter growled. "Goddammit, shit, it's too good."

"Cum for me. Give me everything."

Her orgasm drew closer and her pussy tightened around him as she felt his dick swell. Andy couldn't believe that there was any room for him to grow.

"You have everything that I am, Andy."

The comment brought tears to her eyes. This was a bad idea. But she couldn't stop. He felt too good inside her. His cock slid along her tight walls and made her crazy.

She dropped her right hand to her clit and rubbed. As Hunter pumped into her pussy, her swollen clit begged to be touched. Her body tightened and her head fell back.

"Hunter!" Andy screamed as her release washed over her.

He continued to maneuver her hips over his cock as her juices spilled from her. Her sighs and gasps were loud to her ears, but she didn't care. The eruption washed over her and her hands dropped back to his sides. She clenched his strong hips as another orgasm swam toward her. Her vision blurred and everything went black as the wave crashed over her.

Andy heard Hunter shout her name and his dick pulsated inside her as he found his own release.

Their heavy breathing was harsh as their hips finally slowed and bodies relaxed.

Her hands slid off his sides and her arms fell on the couch. She leaned back, sedate and out of breath. He worshipped her neck with kisses.

She closed her eyes, mind spinning. And not just from the fantastic release she'd just had.

This kind of connection with Hunter was a very bad idea. As the thought formed in her head, he wrapped his arms around her and lowered their bodies onto the couch. He pulled a thin blanket off the back of it and arranged it over them.

Beside him, his arms snug around her, warmth seeped into her bones. She really needed to get up and leave. It would be better to end this now. But her eyelids refused to lift and she couldn't move an inch.

Content to lie there for a few moments, Andy relaxed and listened to his deep breathing. She smiled, pleased that she'd exhausted him as much as he did her.

While his chest rose and fell against her back, a peace she hadn't felt in a long time washed over her. Like a sense of calm that eased her mind and soul.

As sleep tried pulled her under, Andy was too tired to fight the realization that Hunter's face—not Patrick or Peter's—was the last thing on her mind as she surrendered to the darkness.

Chapter Five

"Come in," Andy called after she heard a knock on the door.

"Andy, dear," Mrs. Morrow greeted as she entered the room. "Here's your tea, just how you like it."

The Bed and Breakfast owner was one of Andy's favorite people in the world. Since meeting her the first time when she and Patrick vacationed here on Wolfe Island, the older woman instantly found a place within her heart. The grandmotherly type—now a retired psychologist——she was the perfect hostess who enjoyed taking care of everyone.

Andy always found her easy to love.

"Oh, thank you." Andy placed her clothes in the drawer and reached out to take the tray from her. "You always know just what I need." She placed it on the dresser, then cupped the mug in her hand and waved Mrs. Morrow to sit down. "Have a seat, please. How have you been?"

"I've been fine, just fine." Andy smiled a little as the older woman started fluffing the pillows on the bed instead of taking a seat. Her hostess always had to make sure everything was perfect for her guests. "I'm glad to see you, my dear."

"I'm happy to come back. I had to be here." Andy shook her head and set the mug on the side table. Clenching her fists in her lap, she blew out a shaky breath. "I guess I don't know why the need drove me here but it did."

Mrs. Morrow moved around the bed and sat on the end. "I know what it's like to lose the man you love. It's not easy. Even to this day, I think about my Frederick many times a day. And he's been gone seventeen years."

"You never remarried?"

"Oh heavens no, my dear. He was the only man for me. That I know."

"But," Andy swallowed hard, uncertain how to ask the question, running wild in her mind. "Umm, that's a long time, what about—"

No, she couldn't ask.

Mrs. Morrow chortled. "The look on your face!" She shook her head. "It's okay. Obviously you're thinking about sex."

Andy blushed.

"I said I've never remarried. I didn't say I hadn't found solace in another man's arms now and again. I might be getting on in age but I still know what I need."

"I didn't mean to offend."

"Oh, child, think nothing of it. I don't offend easily. I've had a few men in my life over the years but no one was quite right for me."

Andy nodded. She had a great marriage and Patrick was everything she'd ever wanted in a husband. To be blessed with Peter as well, her life had been perfect.

"If another man came along and made you feel as your husband did, would you consider marrying again?"

"At my age, I'm not sure. I'm seventy-one, my dear, probably too old to get married again."

"But if you did meet a man that you wanted to marry, you would?" Andy persisted.

The older woman's gaze narrowed on her. Andy could practically see the questions churning through the other woman's thoughts.

"I guess it's a possibility. Andy, are you really all right?"

She shook her head, tears filling her eyes. "I'm so lost. Confused. I'm not sure how to move past missing them. It hurts all the time."

Mrs. Morrow reached out for her hand and held it tight. "I'm sorry for everything you've suffered. I know it isn't easy but you have to remember the type of man Patrick was. He would not want you suffering as you are. And that little boy… Oh, Andy, he knew how much you loved him. I didn't have the privilege of meeting him but the love in your voice and eyes when you'd share pictures whenever you were here…oh, that boy would want you to be happy. And have more children someday."

Andy buried her face in her hands and shook with tears. Mrs. Morrow's arm came around her shoulders. "I miss my baby boy so much." Her shoulders shook and the tears fell. The arm around her tightened and held her close.

Once she pulled herself together a bit, Andy lifted her head and laid it on the older woman's shoulder. She savored the warmth and loving touch of a friend.

"I'm not sure I can lay my heart in someone else's hands. No matter how much I believe that he'd take care of it."

"Who is he, Andy?" Mrs. Morrow questioned, her tone soft, without censor.

"Patrick's best friend," Andy whispered.

"That Hunter fellow Patrick mentioned a few times? I remember how much he meant to Patrick."

Andy nodded. "He'd always been family. Peter's godfather, a part of the Sheaver family."

"And how have you felt about him?"

"We've always been friends. In fact," Andy stopped, certain that if she said it out loud, she'd be admitting too much.

"Go on, my dear, your secrets are safe with me."

Andy moved out of her embrace, picked up her tea and held in tight in her hands as she paced the room. "It might be nothing I guess. Back in college, when I first met Hunter, there was an attraction there. God, does that sound awful?"

Mrs. Morrow's hazel eyes met hers. "Did either of you act on the attraction?"

"No, never. I could tell we were both attracted to each another but then I met Patrick. Looking back... Dammit, I don't know. But honestly, I felt safer, more secure with Patrick."

"I see," Mrs. Morrow murmured.

"I'm a horrible person."

"Not at all. Andy." The older woman paused, and patted the seat beside her, beckoning Andy to sit down again. "Listen, you can't regret decisions you made then and you can't change anything now. You must let it all go. You did nothing wrong. Things work out the way they do for many reasons. You loved Patrick wholeheartedly. He knew that. And it is all that matters."

Andy wanted to believe her. In her mind, the words made sense, but in her heart...

It felt as if she'd betrayed Patrick for years by developing deeper feelings for his best friend, to whom she'd once been attracted.

"You need to hear what I'm telling you, Andy. You and Hunter never acted on your feelings for one another, not in your years of marriage to Patrick. It's not like you to cheat. I don't need you to confirm that. You would never have done that to Patrick, to your family. But now, with him gone, wouldn't it be easier for the first relationship you have to be with someone familiar? Someone who has always cared about you?"

Mrs. Morrow's words sunk deep. Andy let them settle and pondered them.

They made sense. Hunter would never do anything to hurt her.

An overwhelming urge to talk to him flooded Andy. She needed to talk to him, figure things out.

She put her arms around her friend and squeezed. "Thank you. You don't know how much you mean to me."

When they pulled apart, they shared a smile.

"I love when you come to visit. I hope our talk has helped?"

"I need to talk to Hunter. Perhaps over the phone, things would be easier?"

The other woman chuckled and patted her shoulder when she stood. "Hmm, don't trust yourself alone with him, do you?" She grinned at Andy over her shoulder when she stood at the door. "I'll see you later, my dear."

After the door closed, Andy grinned. The old woman was coy and perceptive.

She crossed to the bed, pulled her cell phone from her purse and pushed the pillow up against the headboard. She climbed onto the center of the bed and reclined on the pile behind her.

Thanks to Mrs. Morrow's words, she knew the best thing for her was to reach out to Hunter.

She'd made the fast decision to visit the B&B when she'd woken up beside Hunter on the couch at the club five days ago. She'd panicked and needed to reconnect with something familiar that had belonged solely to her and her husband.

Guilt had flooded her. She'd had sex with her husband's best friend. Though it was ridiculous to feel as if she'd betrayed Patrick, her heart had other ideas.

She couldn't allow herself to speculate on what Patrick would think of her. She couldn't regret it. She'd wanted Hunter as much as he had her.

After she'd slid off the couch quietly as possible and gathered her clothing from the floor, she'd quickly dressed, then looked down at Hunter, still sleeping.

He looked so peaceful, face calm and relaxed in sleep. The absent tension in his face after so long was nice to see. The sadness from the last year had eased, and she realized how much pain he'd also been in.

His relationship with Patrick had been strong, without a doubt, and she was angry with herself for being so absorbed in her own pain that she hadn't helped him with his grief.

She'd been such a bitch to Hunter this last year. He'd needed her just as much as she did him. Once it dawned on her how selfish and cold she'd been to him for so long, it was essential to get away from him. How could he even look at her after how horrible she'd been to him?

Scrolling through the contacts on her phone, she pulled up his, took a deep breath, then hit send.

Tapping her fingers on her thigh, she waited nervously for him to answer. After what seemed a dozen rings, she was just about to hang up when she heard his voice. Butterflies fluttered in her belly.

"Hello," she heard him say again.

"Hunter," she said, voice shaking.

"Andy?"

"Yeah, umm, hi."

"Hey, how are you?" She heard the note of concern in his soft voice.

"I'm okay. Is this a bad time?"

"No not at all, I'm working from home for a few days."

"Everything all right at work?" She didn't want to talk about the club, but she didn't know how to start the conversation she knew they needed to have.

"No problems there. Just quieter here, and gives me time to think."

Here's your opening, take it.

"Thinking is good." God, she was such an idiot. Her throat felt tight and dry. The words were stuck in her throat.

His chuckle wafted over the line. "Sure. Listen, Andy, I can hear the nerves in your voice so I'm going to cut right to the chase of things. I've left you dozens of messages over the last few days, since I woke up to find you gone. Are you all right? Really?"

She remembered the texts he'd sent that she hit ignore on. He cared about her. She should have been a better friend, if he considered her even that now, and let him know she was okay.

"I'm sorry, I needed some space. I should have replied."

"All right. I understand what you're going through, too. He was my best friend. To be with you like that wasn't an easy decision for me, either."

"It didn't seem too difficult when you threw that ultimatum at me." Andy said, anger seeping into her a bit. He'd pushed her, forced things between them to take a different path.

She had to wonder if her anger was because she'd wanted him. For years, the attraction she'd once felt for him lay smothered and forgotten. In the moment he threw down the gauntlet, the attraction had resurfaced and she was forced to face it.

"I'm sorry, I shouldn't have said that."

"No, you have every reason to be angry. The heat of the moment, concern about the path you were on… Hell, Andy, I didn't know how else to stop you. I care about you."

Her skin tingled at the gruffness in his voice. "I know. It's difficult for me not to feel guilty, like I betrayed Patrick."

He sighed. "I understand. But if there's one thing— and I've said it before—Patrick would have wanted is for you to live again. It's not your fault, no way at all."

Tears filled her eyes as she leaned back. "How can I ask for any type of happiness when I lost my little boy and caused his father so much pain? Hunter…"

"You have to know that no one but you can make your decisions. And no one but you is blaming you for what happened. Life happens as it does. We learn from it. Pick ourselves up and move forward. I miss them too. Every day I want to call my best friend and tell him something about business or whatever, but I can't."

Andy swallowed. She knew his pain but never allowed herself to think of anyone else suffering as much as she was. Had never thought to care about how he was feeling. She had stopped being there for him. But he'd never stopped wanting to be there for her.

"I'm not sure how to find myself again," she admitted.

"I can't tell you how to move forward, but will say that you start by reconciling yourself to the fact that nothing is your fault. You have many loved ones around you who care about you. And support you. You're not alone."

"A step at a time."

"Exactly, that's all you can do. There's no pressure here."

She smiled. "No more ultimatums?"

"Well, depends on what the choices are. And how tough I have to be."

The conversation shifted, as did the tone of his husky voice. She shivered and her nipples beaded. Dammit, she had to pull herself together. This wasn't why she'd called him.

She coughed to clear her throat. "How you make me feel scares the hell out of me." Her eyes widened, she wanted to recall the words as soon as she left her mouth. They weren't what she expected.

"Trust me, the feeling is mutual," he said, gruff and soft. "But I've had longer to live with mine. Why don't you tell me more? What do I make you feel?"

She frowned, confused by his *"I've had longer"* comment, but pushed it aside, thinking he wasn't saying things correctly.

"Weak in the knees, I guess."

"Hmm, and...?" he asked.

"Very cared for."

"That's a given."

"Like I have a friend who will always be here for me."

"Most definitely."

"Sexy," she whispered.

"You are most definitely sexy. Stunning, really."

"You're biased," she chuckled.

"No, just honest."

"Thank you."

"When will I get to see you?" he demanded.

She frowned. "Are you okay?"

"Yes, I just would rather have this conversation in person. To tell you how gorgeous you are face-to-face. Maybe show you."

Andy shifted on the bed, goosebumps spread along her skin. To take things with him to the next level...was she ready? She needed just a bit more time.

"I'll be home in a few days."

"Home? Where the hell are you?"

"Wolfe Island. I needed some space."

He sighed. She pictured him running his hand through his hair in frustration, like she'd seen him do many times.

"How much longer will you be gone?"

She picked at the small piece of lint on the quilt. "I don't know for sure, but maybe three or four more days."

"Will you come see me the minute you're home? I need to hold you, Andy," he whispered.

"Hunter," she breathed, body shaking with need and yearning.

"Dammit, don't sound like that and expect me to just sit here and wait. Promise me you'll be no more than three or four days. I can't do this on the phone and not come for you."

That he would sweep in here, find her and take her in his arms…

Her body ignited and juices gathered between her thighs.

"Four days at the most, I promise. I'll see you soon."

"I miss you, Andy," he murmured.

She was helpless to deny him. "I miss you, too."

She heard the click in her ear and hung up. Enough had been said. She laid her cell on the bed beside her and curled up on her side.

A smile played on her lips, knowing he was thinking about her in this moment too.

Though she wanted to rush back home and find him, she still needed a few days to remember the past and make certain she was ready for the future. Whatever it might be.

There would be no turning back once she was in Hunter's arms again.

She suspected he would never let her go.

And she wasn't sure she'd be able to walk away either.

****

Andy set the last of the folded laundry on her bed.

She'd never been so exhausted in her life. The emotions over the last few days had taken a toll on her. Taking the trip to Wolfe Island had been a great idea but the drive tiring.

She wanted to hurry to Hunter's door, but needed to acclimate herself to being home again.

But she wanted to be certain that she wasn't just reacting to being lonely. She needed to prove that even while in the house she'd shared with Patrick, she could have the overwhelming urgency to see Hunter...

The fact was proven. She'd missed him more than she ever thought she would. Hell, even while tending to menial tasks, he was continually on her mind.

Andy turned away from the laundry, her heart still aching for all she'd lost, and for the time she'd wasted closing herself off from those that cared about her.

Walking the short distance to the end bedroom, she stood in front of the closed cherry wood door.

Andy traced the letters of Peter's name that he'd proudly helped her hang on the door. He'd been so excited to see his name in different colors and call it his.

With a deep breath, she grabbed the doorknob, and opened the door.

Her eyes filled with tears as she crossed the threshold into her son's dinosaur domain.

Dinosaur wallpaper covered the walls, curtains her mother-in-law had made with fabric she'd searched far and wide for—just so he could have his favorite prehistoric animal on them—hung on the window. To match the curtains, Jeanine also used the same fabric to make the comforter and bedding. Peter had been ecstatic to see the Allosaurus, T-Rex and Stegosaurus everywhere. She and Patrick had shopped endlessly for every dinosaur stuffed animal and toy they could find.

Andy swallowed hard and sat in the rocking chair in front of the window. She laid her head back and set the rocker in motion. With a deep breath, the blueberry scent her son loved to use in his baths carried into this room, and lingered still. The distinct fragrance washed over her. She smiled.

Tears slid down her cheeks as she laughed aloud, thinking about her son.

Peter filled her heart with his laughter and pleasure in life.

She sobered. She'd done so wrong by him.

Instead of pushing through the pain that losing him caused, she'd wallowed in grief and became someone even she didn't know. She should have honored his and his father's memories by dealing with the pain and finding the strength to move forward.

She should have done something to make sure neither of their deaths was for nothing. She could have joined MADD, sought out other parents who suffered the loss of a child, other woman aching without their husbands.

But she'd done none of that. She was angry with herself for the waste she'd allowed her own life to become. To turn her back on the charities that had counted on her, the love she'd had in her life.

But she needed the time to heal. To be alone and work through the grief in her own way. She just never intended to shut herself off so completely from those who cared for her and counted on her.

Andy looked around the room.

She needed to get her life back. To find the pleasures in life again that she'd always enjoyed. The family she still had in the Sheavers, her parents who were hundreds of miles away but still with her all the time.

And Hunter.

The love he had for her little boy. An uncle and godfather who'd loved him as if he was his own. Andy loved that about him.

Yes, she loved Hunter. Deeply.

He was everything she admired in a man—strong, supportive, kind and thoughtful, goal-oriented and sexy to boot. He'd be a wonderful father as well.

While different from what she'd felt for Patrick, her love for Hunter was just as strong.

Patrick had been everything to her, and would always love him.

To find a second love in her life was more than she could ever have hoped for. It was more than most people experienced.

It was time to move on and make something great out of the life she still had. Patrick would have wanted it for her. She would have wanted the same for him if roles were reversed. She would never want him to be alone or fall into a dark pit of despair that did more harm than good.

Down deep, there would always be some of the guilt over losing the two people she'd loved most. But she needed to honor them by being the strong, resilient woman they could be proud of.

And she'd hold on tight to new love. It was time to start over.

Andy stood and moved across the room. She ran her fingers over the comforter on Peter's bed as she walked by. At the doorway, she turned and gazed around the room once again.

"I love you, buddy. Know that Mommy will always love you with all her heart."

She closed the door behind her and leaned her head back against it. Tears fell down her cheeks even as she smiled and the heaviness in her heart alleviated.

New plans formed in Andy's mind. Giddy over what the future held and the decisions she'd made, she headed to the kitchen in search of a pad and pen.

She had to get her plans on paper for the future.

Chapter Six

Andy rang the doorbell, heart pounding hard in her chest and waited. She hoped Hunter was home. He'd mentioned working from home for a few days and she hadn't considered calling ahead.

The door swung open and he stood before her. Jeans and t-shirt, no socks...he looked spectacular.

"Hello, Hunter," she greeted, her body on fire.

Damn he was sexy as hell.

"Can I come in?"

Wordlessly, his grey eyes turned smoky as they swept over her, and he stepped back.

She crossed the threshold and closed the door behind her.

Leaning against it, she stared at him. "I'm so glad to see you," she whispered.

He moved quickly, as if he had been waiting for some sign of encouragement. His body bracketed hers against the door and his head swooped low. His soft lips moved over hers gently, brushed against hers in the sweetest way.

Their first kiss.

Her heart pitched, realizing it was true. She could kick herself for withholding such an experience from herself. He tasted minty and delicious.

She hadn't been kissed or held like this in forever. To have a man hold her gently, as if he cherished her dearly...she was blessed.

Her mouth opened against his, her tongue brushing his bottom lip. Hunter pulled back with a groan. Andy shivered as she looked into his eyes. Yearning and fire blazed from within. He wanted her, and she relished it.

"Umm, maybe we should talk," he suggested, but then leaned in and gave her another quick kiss on the lips. "Really, there's so much to say."

"Hunter," Andy began and laid a hand on his chest.

"Andy, look. I can't stay here with you like this. I want you." He groaned when her fist clenched and grazed his nipple beneath his shirt. "Dammit."

"It's okay, just relax," she implored.

"No, it isn't." He grabbed her hand and put it down over the front of his pants. His cock was hard and jerked at her touch.

"Oh," she breathed.

"Yes, oh." Hunter chuckled, though she heard the strain in it. "It's just what happens when you're near me. One night was not enough."

Andy's hand stilled over his cock. It twitched against her palm. She really needed to give him some space. But she really just wanted him to kiss her again.

"No, one night was not enough. And neither was just one kiss," she whispered, cupping the back of his neck and pulled his head down to hers. Her mouth claimed his this time, tongue plundering. They both groaned.

Hunter's arms tightened around her. He held her tight as their tongues tangled and they breathed one another in.

His mouth eased away, and reined kisses everywhere along her neck he could reach. "I'm having a hard time resisting you," he whispered in her ear.

Andy trembled, her fingers clenched around his biceps. "Hunter…" she gushed out, certain if he let go of her right now, she'd fall in a heap on the floor. His teeth grazed her neck, and she gasped.

"One step at a time, sweetheart." Hunter groaned and shifted back a bit.

Their gazes locked and her hold on him tightened. Suddenly, taking things slow didn't seem all that realistic.

Their chemistry was too strong. She needed to be with him, like this, and was helpless to resist.

"How about a new deal?" she whispered.

Hunter's gaze narrowed.

"Don't look at me like that." She chuckled. "I didn't think about this one step at a time business very clearly. I want you. Now."

His eyes darkened. "Deal," he accepted, then slid an arm under her knees and one at her back and scooped her up.

She tilted her head back and giggled. "You don't need to think about it?"

Hunter growled, "Hell no, I don't need to think about it. But we're not doing this here."

Andy held on tight as he walked through the living room, down the hall and through the door on the right. He carried her over to the king-sized bed and set her on the edge of it. He left her there, moved to the side table and clicked on a small lamp that cast the room in a light orange glow.

Her gaze never left him as he lifted his blue t-shirt and pulled it over his head. He came back to her and stood before her. Her head tilted. He smiled.

"I've dreamt about you many times in this bed," he admitted softly.

Her nipples tightened. She grinned, then lifted her hands to his belt buckle. "Was I doing this?" She made quick work of unbuckling the belt, undoing the button of his jeans and easing the zipper down.

"You've done it a time or two," he said gruffly.

"Mmm, nice." She eased her fingers into the waistband and pushed the jeans down his hips. His cock bobbed in front of her, stiff and swollen. Once his pants were at his knees, Andy cupped his fine ass in her palms. Hunter groaned.

She smirked up at him, then lightly blew against his flesh. His hands lifted and pulled her hair back as her breath washed over his cock. Inch by inch, she moved closer to him, squeezing his ass cheeks while she blew again and watched his cock jerk.

She pulled back. "What else have I done in your dreams?" she murmured, grinning.

"Andy," he moaned and tried to step away.

"Stay," she demanded and held him in place. Her fingers clenched his ass. "Did I do this?"

Before he could object or try to move again, Andy lowered her head and licked the head of his dick. His hands fisted her hair and he blew out a ragged breath.

Fueled and feeling wicked, Andy ran her tongue up and down his length, hands cradling his ass. She'd never hesitated when it came to sex, but with Hunter, she felt even more bold and daring.

She fisted his shaft, then pushed her mouth over his entire length. She suckled him a moment, then pushed down onto him farther. Hunter huffed as she took him deep until his cock touched the back of her throat.

Andy inhaled, then pulled back, and repeated the movements a dozen more times. Her mouth worked over him. His guttural groans filled her with pleasure.

He pushed the sweater off her shoulders as she took him deep once more. Fists clenched, he jerked back. His cock popped out of her mouth and her hands fell away from him.

"Hey." Her protest was cut off as Hunter tossed the sweater over his shoulder as his lips met hers. His tongue violated her mouth.

She moaned and started to fall back onto the bed, but his hands grasped the hem of her shirt and tugged it over her head, then let her fall.

Hunter's chest heaved as he looked down at her. She shifted, then leaned back on her elbows so he could see all of her.

Sliding her hands behind her back, she undid the clasp of her bra. She left it there over her breasts, teasing him a little.

Hunter lowered his body over her, his lips on hers again. Softer this time, he caressed hers with an open-mouthed kiss. Her strength gave out and she fell back. Her arms wrapped around his shoulders and returned his kiss with vigor. He was an amazing kisser.

She shivered as his fingers feathered along her sides and up to her breasts. He removed her yellow bra and withdrew his mouth from hers. Andy breathed in deep as he lifted himself up, his arm muscles bulging as he looked down at her.

"You are beautiful, Andy," he murmured, gaze serious. "I can't believe you're here."

She reached up, ran her hands over his glorious chest. "I don't want you to fuck me, Hunter."

His body jerked as if punched, and his smile faded.

Unwavering, she whispered, "I want you to make love to me." Her palms slid over his shoulders and down his chest as she smiled up at him. He grinned.

She reached down to the button of her pants and undid them. Hunter stepped back, grabbed the top of her khakis and pulled them down her hips.

Naked, she lay still, arms over her head, and let him look his fill. He stood between her spread legs, the fire and hunger in his eyes warming her as they roamed over her body.

Andy's breath caught. He made her feel so cherished and beautiful. And her pussy tingled as he stroked himself before her. He was gorgeous, head to toe.

And all hers.

Palms flat on the bed, she shoved her body backward, sliding along the comforter until she reached the middle. She pushed the pillows off the bed, and raised her arms toward him.

He crawled up the bed without hesitation. She spread her legs for him, her arms wrapped around his back as he covered her. Their lips met, gently brushing against each other as he found his spot between her thighs. His dick nudged her opening. She clutched him closer.

Hunter held her head as his tongue dived into her mouth, dueling with hers. Her hands slid down his back to his ass. She widened her legs and pressed his hips tighter into hers. He lifted his head and gazed down at her.

"Andy, sweetheart," he whispered as his cock nudged inside her. Her hips came off the bed as his arched.

A thrill swept through her as his hard, straight cock, entered her with no restriction. His hips dropped and seated his shaft inside her. Andy gasped, surprised at the ease and unexpected rush of him being inside her.

Hunter closed his eyes and groaned. Neither moved. Their breathing was the only sound in the room. His lids lifted and he looked down at her.

He slid his fingers from her hair and down her cheek. His eyes were soft, loving and heated. Tears filled her own.

"Sweetheart…" Hunter began.

Andy smiled, and tried desperately not to move her hips. She loved the feel of him seated inside her. She could lie like this forever.

"It's okay, it's just…" Emotions overwhelmed her. She had no idea how to put what she felt it into words.

Hunter brushed his lips against hers, then pulled back.

Andy huffed, surprised. His hips moved again, pushing even deeper inside her. She panted, and the rush of pleasure swept through her as he filled her over and over again.

"I know, sweetheart. I know," Hunter whispered above her. "Being inside you like this is a dream come true. Christ," He swore and angled his hips. Hers arched higher as his cock hit deeper.

"Hunter," she gushed, feeling as if there was no air for her to breathe. She let herself go and just lived in the moment. This man, this amazing friend-turned-lover, was all she could ever want inside her.

Making love with him was more than she could ever imagine. She felt alive in his arms.

"I'm going to love you every day for as long as you'll let me." Hunter's gaze bore into her, determined and full of promise.

Andy lifted her legs and wrapped them tight around his waist. He moaned his approval and plunged deep.

Their lips met. Every gasp and moan shared.

Andy hadn't felt this free in so long. She was learning to live again, letting herself heal. There would be no more longing for pain to drown out her guilt. Only Hunter taking care of her, loving her.

Andy wrenched her mouth from his and shouted as her orgasm took over. Swept away in the tide, she trembled and clung to him.

She heard Hunter's harsh shout from a distance. Her ears rang and her heart beat rapidly. Tears fell down Andy's cheeks as happiness bloomed inside her. As her mind settled and body relaxed, her hold tightened on the man above her.

"You're everything I could want," she whispered.

He buried his face in her neck and sighed. She felt the smile spread across his face against her skin.

Yes, she knew he loved her, and she was already well on her way to being deeply in love with him.

But Andy withheld the words. Her hands roamed his back and pinched his ass. He drew back and looked down at her, the biggest smile on his face she'd ever seen. Still, the words wouldn't come.

Those words had only been said to one man in her life.

She wasn't quite ready to say it to a second.

****

Hunter stood in the doorway of his bedroom, glass of water in his hand, and frowned. Andy had been curled up, cuddled in his bedding when he'd left her.

Making love with her, finally admitting how much he cared about her…his life would never be the same. She still needed time, though. And adjust to the idea of making changes in her life. He'd give her the time to get used to things, but he'd be right alongside her the whole way.

Smiling, he turned and headed toward his den. He hadn't passed her in the living room on his way back from the kitchen and the bathroom door was open. There was only one other room she could be.

His smiled died when he stood in the doorway and noticed the tears on her pale face.

Standing by his desk, her gaze was fixated on the mantle over his fireplace.

His "family" pictures sitting on top were probably a surprise to her. Andy had only been to his condo a few times, either to pick up Peter when Hunter babysat after a date-night with Patrick, or to drop something off. She'd never once been in his den.

The pictures ranged in size: the largest was an eleven by fourteen of Peter on his fourth birthday. Chocolate cake covered both his cheeks and his hands had mushed even more between his fingers. Peter loved chocolate cake, and Andy had always made him his very own small, one-layer cake that he would have all to himself. The picture was one of Hunter's favorites.

Framed eight by tens and five by sevens held so many memories, and those he loved embraced him whenever he walked into his office.

He took a step toward her, but she held up her hand to stop him, then wiped the tears from her cheeks. Her gaze swung toward him, and he swallowed hard.

He understood seeing the pictures had to be hard for her, especially since her home was void of memories like this. But he would not deal with the pain as she had. He wanted the physical memories around him, to feel the love he had for the people most important to him. This way, he couldn't hide from the pain.

He held his hand out, but she turned away and walked to the mantle.

She lifted the large photo of Peter and ran a finger down the glass, as if touching her little boy's cheek.

"I could have beaten you with the toy gun you got him that day." Andy's voice was so soft he could barely hear her so he shifted closer. "He pulled that trigger at every opportunity. It made so much noise."

Hunter smiled and laid an elbow on the end of the stone. "Every boy needs to have a toy plastic gun," he joked.

Andy's brow arched. "Couldn't find one that was silent, though, could you?"

"Nah, of course not. The noisier, the better."

She pulled the frame to her chest and hugged it tight. "He had so much fun that day. The older he got, the more he loved his birthday." She looked down at the picture again, then back at Hunter. "I love this picture."

"Maybe you should consider getting some of your photos out again," Hunter offered casually. "Remember that one of him and Patrick, the first time we all took him to the beach? That was a priceless one. I still remember Peter's face when Patrick had dipped his feet into the water." Hunter shook his head and smiled. "I'd never seen anyone with such a red face of fear and tears falling down his cheeks."

Andy laughed softly. "Yes. Remember Patrick's reaction?" She placed the frame gently back on the shelf. "You'd think he'd just stabbed his son with a pin. He was so upset that he'd scared Peter."

Hunter loved hearing her carefree laugh again. He hadn't heard it in so long.

"You know, you might be right." Andy picked up the smaller picture of Hunter, Patrick, Jeanine and Tony.

"I'm always right." Hunter grinned. "Haven't you figured that out yet?"

Andy swatted his arm. "I'm serious. Maybe I should get some of those pictures out again."

Hunter's heart swelled with love and surprise. Maybe the time away had given her some freedom, and not being in the house alone may have helped.

He walked to the old sofa against the wall and sat on one end. The faded brown couch had followed him from his first apartment over the bar where he worked, then to college and now to the first home he'd bought. Patrick would tease him about the "hunk of junk" as he'd called it, about it being the only ugly thing Hunter owned.

But he could never get rid of it. It had survived a lot with him.

He watched as Andy continued to pick up and gaze at each photo. Her long, brown tresses obscured most of her face from sight, but he saw her wheels turning. With each small hitch of her breath or smile, he knew she was reliving memories.

A photo in hand, Andy turned and approached him. She sat beside him, close enough to touch but not crowding him. She turned the frame around for him to see. "I like this one a lot." She smiled.

The photo of her holding Peter, with him and Patrick on each side of her looking down at the baby, was one of his favorites, too.

Hunter treasured the photos he was in with the Sheavers or with Andy, Patrick and Peter. Nothing meant more to him than the five people who loved him unconditionally. He smiled and nodded. "It's a fantastic picture."

She stared down at it, then set it on the small table in front of her. She shifted to get more comfortable and leaned back against the sofa. "You meant so much to Patrick. You were the brother he always wanted."

His throat tightened. His bond with Patrick had been that of brothers. Hearing her say it, now, when he missed his buddy so much, choked him up. He cleared his throat. "I thought of him the same way."

"You took care of one another." Andy breathed out a small laugh. "I would sometimes get jealous of how much time the two of you spent together and even finished one another's sentences."

Hunter gaped at her. "You didn't have anything to be jealous about."

She shrugged, her cheeks red. "I know, it sounds silly, but those were things he and I should have been doing."

Hunter shook his head, unsure what to say. "I'm sorry…"

She clasped his hand from where it laid on the couch. "Oh no, don't apologize. Trust me, it's fine. I got over it, and the more you were around and I got to know you, I couldn't help but understand. Besides, a husband and wife can't share everything all the time now can they."

She didn't really pose it as a question so Hunter remained silent and wondered where her thoughts were headed.

"Did you know the only real fight we ever had was about you?"

What the hell…? "What do you mean? What was the fight about?" Hunter wasn't sure he truly wanted to know.

They were all his family. He hated the thought that he'd imposed too much and caused a problem between Andy and Patrick.

"Seems silly to think about it now, but remember when Patrick wanted to take that ski trip to Vermont?"

Hunter nodded.

"He wanted it to be a weekend for us alone. He'd promised it would be." She continued, and Hunter's heart sank. He knew what trip she meant. "Of course you didn't know he'd promised me, but you showed up the next morning and told him the renovations to the club were complete. It would open the next week."

Her gaze met his. "Patrick was thrilled for you. He was so excited; it was as if it were his club. And right on the spot, he…"

"Asked me to go to Vermont to celebrate," Hunter filled in, embarrassed. His hand tightened on hers.

"Yep, just like that. It was also the weekend I wanted to tell him I was pregnant." She chuckled. "I ended up blurting it out over dinner the first night there. I was so angry with him. I thought it would serve him right."

"Andy, I didn't know."

"I know. And we ended up having an even better time the rest of the weekend. You were both ecstatic. Hunter…" She stopped, maybe hesitant.

Hunter reached out and lifted her face with a finger on her chin. "Tell me."

She clasped his hand in hers and held it against her knees. He shifted closer.

"You were there my entire marriage." Her fingers covered his mouth, silencing him when he tried to speak. "You were there for everything. And it's okay. In a very weird and strange way, one which doesn't fully make sense to me, losing Patrick angered and made me sad for various reasons."

Hunter scowled. "What do you mean?" he asked, from behind her fingers.

Her hand lowered and wrapped around his again.

"I was angry that I'd lost both of them. The two people I loved most in the world were just gone. And I have been angry with God and everyone around me for still being here. But I've come to realize I was angry because you'd also lost them." Her eyes watered and she gave herself a small shake. "You, who were an amazing uncle, brother, needed them as much as I did. It made me angry that we'd both lost them. You know my parents have always travelled and rarely ever remember that they have a child. We're similar in so many ways, you and I. I never really noticed it before. But Peter and Patrick were *ours*. Why did we have to lose them?" Andy drew in a harsh breath.

Hunter couldn't fight it any longer. He pulled her into his arms. She was right. They had lost the two people most important to them and never grieved together.

Sobs racked their bodies as they allowed themselves to let go. Hunter had never realized he hadn't grieved as he probably should have.

When he felt Andy's sobs lessen and his own had stopped, he pulled back and wiped at his cheeks. He cupped her face in his hands and thumbed her tears away. Leaning forward, he kissed her on the nose.

"Thank you," he said gently. "I didn't realize how much I needed to grieve like that. Especially with you. Besides Tony and Jeanine, no one else truly understands what the last year has been like."

She nodded. "You're right. I talked to them on the phone before I came here."

He was glad she had remained close with the Sheavers even though she'd believed they blamed her for the losses they all shared. They loved her as much as he did.

Desperate to pledge his love to her forever but certain she wasn't ready to hear it, he shifted uncomfortably.

"Do you want anything, Andy? Something to drink?" Hunter stood, desperate to hide his true feelings.

She looked up at him, arms folded in front of her. "Running, Hunter? That's not like you."

He speared her with a glare. "I'm not running. I just thought we'd expended enough deep emotion today. You obviously don't agree."

He turned toward his desk, needing to keep his hands busy. When Andy's hand grabbed his wrist, he knew she wasn't going to let up. As much as he wanted to discuss the future, fear of it made him want to avoid it. But they had to resolve their issues in order to move on.

Hunter's heart hurt at the thought of moving on and not loving her as she should be loved.

****

Her heart racing, Andy's hand tightened around Hunter's wrist.

She'd come to see him in order to clear the air and find out if they could say the things that really needed to be said, in order to figure out the future.

But their desire for one another had kicked in immediately and neither resisted. She'd wanted him—on top, under, behind her—any way possible, as long as he was touching her.

Ecstasy in his arms was unbelievable. She was always a needy lover, but gave back as good as she got, and he met her stroke for stroke.

"Come sit back down, please," she requested softly.

He hesitated when she tugged on his arm, but finally relented. She ran her hands over the couch and really looked at it for the first time.

"This must be the hideous brown *"better in the garbage"* couch Patrick told me about," she commented.

Hunter sat and frowned. "It's been with me for years. I can't part with it."

Though she'd tried to lighten the mood, Hunter sat rigid, his gaze averted.

"Sometimes we need certain things in our lives that no one else understands." Andy hesitated, then took a deep breath. "Like you. I want you in my life more now than ever. I should never have taken my pain out on you. Made you feel worse than you were already feeling."

Hunter's gaze widened and his jaw clenched. He nodded. "I need your friendship in my life, too."

The poor man. He looked so dejected Andy had to keep herself from chuckling.

"That's not what I meant."

He tilted his head and frowned. "No?"

She shifted closer until their knees touched. She laid a hand over his. "For the last year you've been there for me. I might not have wanted you to be, but you were. And the last six months…" She paused and shook her head sadly. "You've pushed me to get back among the living. Even if it was to go out and get my hair done. You wouldn't allow me to curl up and waste away. I fought you every step of the way."

"You think?" Hunter smirked.

She squeezed his knee and pointed her index finger at him. "Don't be a smartass. The point is you took care of me. Hell, I would never have groceries in the house if it wasn't for you bringing some by. I really let my grief take over my life. I want you to know, as I told Tony and Jeanine, I'm not going to live like that any longer."

Hunter tucked her hair behind her ear. She thought her heart would thud out of her chest.

"That's great news. I'm sure you'll find all the strength you need to make it happen."

"I think I will." She looked over at the photos lining his mantle, then back at him. "I will forever miss them. Peter will always be my first child and that void in my heart will never be full again. And I love Patrick. He'll always be with me. We shared some of the very best years of my life. He was my everything, you know that, right?"

She looked at him, imploringly, hoping he understood.

Hunter shifted, then nodded. "Yes, I know. He was your one great love. The two of you were wonderful together."

"Until I pulled myself out of the dark and agonizing place I was in, I would have agreed with you that he was my one great love. But I've come to learn that maybe there's more than one love for everyone."

He shook his head. "Patrick was your soul mate. I've heard you say it a million times over the years."

She nodded; frustrated with herself that she wasn't explaining it to him well. He didn't get it. "Yes, I do think he was my soul mate, but I don't think he'll be the only one in my life."

Hunter's eyes bulged. Andy nearly laughed. He looked as if his eyes were about to pop out of his gorgeous head.

"You mean you're going to start…dating?"

She chuckled. "Don't sound so shocked. But no, I'm not going to start dating." She took a deep breath and forged on. "I'm already seeing someone."

"What the fuck? Andy, we just…when…"

Andy pushed him back into the corner of the couch when she realized he was about to bolt off it, anger pouring off him. She should have worded things better. "No, relax. Let me finish."

"I don't believe it. I'll kill him!" Hunter's fists clenched at his sides.

"Hunter, look at me." She cupped his cheek. "Don't be dense. I'm talking about you, you dolt. I want to see where you and I will lead."

His body jerked. "You mean," he swallowed, "you and I are dating?"

She nodded and dropped her arm. Nervousness zipped through her body. "Yes, if you want to. I know we kind of started backward. The night at the club, earlier." She paused then said, "It was amazing. As much as I tried to keep things impersonal, you still wormed your way into my heart. It was as if that night, I allowed myself to open up." Her gaze met his. "Your presence in my life, in my heart, blossomed into the realization of how important you are to me."

His hand clasped hers tight. "You deserve better than finding some guy to have sex with who will never treat you like a lady should be treated. That night, today, meant more to me than you know."

Deep inside, Andy knew Hunter had always loved her as more than a friend. But until the words left his mouth, she wouldn't put him on the spot. He'd kept his feelings to himself and allowed Patrick his happiness. He'd been true family to Patrick. His selflessness made her adore him even more.

"I'd love us to take it one step at a time. I trust you. I don't know what the future holds for us, Hunter." She wanted—needed—him to know that more than anything.

Andy couldn't say for certain where they'd be in three, six or a thousand months, but she did love him. They'd started as great friends and had become so much more. The time away made her see things so much more clearly. But she still wanted more time to heal and truly forgive herself for everything.

Hunter smiled and pulled her toward him. She laid her head on his shoulder as he wrapped his arms around her and cuddled her close.

"One step at a time it is." He tucked a finger under her chin, and she leaned her head back. "We don't have to rush anything."

Andy looked deep into his eyes. They were alight with joy and his smile was contagious. "No, we don't need to rush anything."

"We'll simply be together. I'd love to take you to dinner. Just the two of us," he suggested.

Andy suddenly realized the once bright room had darkened now that the sun went down. Her stomach growled, which caused them both to laugh.

Her head back in the crook of his arm, she cupped his cheek. "Dinner sounds wonderful." She grinned.

Chapter Seven

Five months later…
Andy rolled over and cracked one eye open. Groaning, she quickly shut out the harsh light and buried her head back in the pillow.

She'd been up late the night before, going over the new architectural plans she had for her house, reorganizing her schedule for upcoming charity events and had a bit too much wine with a couple of friends. She hadn't seen them in ages and loved reconnecting. It was difficult to convince herself that it was okay to spend an evening out, laughing and enjoying life again. Thanks to Hunter, she was making the slow progression back to what she loved to do and not feel guilty doing so.

Hunter.

She burrowed beneath the blankets and smiled. He really made her feel good about where she was heading, and treasured her completely, always looking after her while also giving her space to find solid footing again.

"Hey, sleepyhead, rise and shine," the voice cooed, jarring her from her thoughts.

She lifted her head and raised an arm to block out the sunshine pouring in from the bay window of his bedroom.

"Oh, sorry, let me get that." The room darkened after he pulled the curtains closed and turned back to her.

Her gaze clear, it zeroed in on him and ran the length of his body. She never grew tired of seeing him. His strong arms, long fingers, solid chest—she savored being cocooned against him whenever he pulled her near, or if he could see the doubts shadowing her eyes.

"You're awfully cheery this morning."

"Of course I am." He moved to the end of the bed and lifted a tray she hadn't noticed, and sat down. Once he set it down between them, she was surprised to see chocolate covered strawberries and two flutes of what might be apple cider on top.

"What's all this?"

"Don't you know what today is?" he questioned, eyes twinkling.

God she could drown in their depths and never come out. He was spectacular.

"Umm, Friday?" she frowned, totally at a loss.

He chuckled and handed her a glass. "Yes, it's Friday, but even better, it's our fifth month together." Grinning, he clinked his glass with hers and took a sip.

Eyes wide, she pondered. An anniversary, so to speak. It seemed surreal. When she'd decided to pull herself up by her boot straps and learn to live again, she'd taken each day as it came. And never planned too far ahead.

To know the time had flown by without her being aware felt strange, considering she'd once wallowed in grief so heavy she barely made it through a day without hiding.

But it was also exciting.

"Oh, I'm sorry, I didn't—" He laid his fingers over her lips to silence her.

Hunter gazed into her eyes, lowered his hand, then lightly brushed her lips with his. "Don't worry about it. I figured you'd forgotten but that didn't mean I had to." He winked and picked up a strawberry.

He placed it against her lips. Her mouth opened and she bit into the sweet morsel. Tangy, sweet nectar and the richness of chocolate coated her tongue. She moaned and her eyes nearly rolled back in her head.

She stared at the man beside her and palmed his cheek. "You're spoiling me."

"That's what I'm here for. And I told you, don't worry about it. I simply wanted to enjoy the morning with you and see how you're doing."

"I'm fine." She set the glass on the bedside table and reclined against the headboard, pillows behind her back.

"I know you're doing fine, but you've been very busy lately. I want to be sure you're not doing more than you feel comfortable with because you think it's expected of you."

She shook her head. "No, I'm doing just fine. I enjoy organizing the charity events again. You know I've always loved doing those."

He shifted, and moved the tray to the floor, then settled on his side facing her.

He always made her feel special, and she needed to plan something in return. Every day with him was amazing. They were inseparable for the most part.

They hadn't told the Sheavers about their relationship yet. Fast-talking, keeping things quiet and controlling themselves whenever the older couple was around, was taking its toll.

Though Andy desperately wanted to tell her ex in-laws about her relationship with Hunter, she was worried how they might react.

They had been there for her since his death, even when she tried to push them away. To know she'd moved on, and with his best friend, might not go over so well with either of them. Their allegiance would always be to their son's memory. She only hoped they would understand.

"Hey, where'd you go?" Hunter pulled her from her thoughts.

"I'm right here." She lifted a hand to his chest and absorbed the feel of him against her skin. Warm, hard, tight…damn she loved touching him.

Pulling her closer, his lips captured hers, sliding and caressing. The taste of strawberries was rich on his tongue. It slid along hers, his teeth biting at her bottom lip. Her toes curled, and her fingers tightened around his ears.

He eased back, panting, and cuddled her close. "Damn, you're potent."

She chuckled and tried to get closer still. No matter how close he lay against her, sometimes she needed to feel him against her even more. He was so much more to her than she ever thought she'd find again.

His love was amazing.

Thanks to the man in her arms, she understood that in loving someone again, and opening herself was the best thing she could ever do for either of them.

There would come a time when she'd walk alongside the two loves she'd lost again. But for now, she found a love she couldn't live without.

"This probably isn't the best time to bring this up since you're lying in bed with me and we could be all kinds of naughty," She giggled and brushed her lips over his then pulled back. "But how about in a few weeks we talk to Tony and Jeanine, and tell them we're together?"

"Are you sure?" He slid a finger down her nose, making her heart skip a beat. She'd come to love the small quirky gesture of his.

"Yes. I think it's time. They'll be back from their vacation in about three to four weeks. We'll tell them as soon as possible once they're back. Maybe Thanksgiving."

Hunter's eyes widened but he nodded. "Deal." Lowering his head, his lips claimed hers again. He tugged the sheet away from her body.

His gaze roamed her near-naked form, hands following. She purred, easing back, an arm lifted over her head as he explored.

Each bit of flesh he touched caused sparks to flare to life, making her skin heat. Fingers like magic, he'd learned every inch of her quickly during their time together. Now a master at making her body, heart and soul sing for him, she was helpless to resist him.

"You're exquisite," he whispered, his lips pecking a line across her stomach.

Her muscles quivered as juices pooled between her thighs. Pushing a hand through his spiky, jet-black hair, she watched as he lavished her body with attention.

"I will never, ever get enough of you." He looked up at her, the truth of his words conveyed in the depths of his eyes.

She loved him for always being honest with her. Always being who he was—her friend and lover—never rushing her.

How'd she'd gotten so lucky twice in one lifetime, she'd never understand.

But she'd definitely hang on with both hands and enjoy him to the fullest.

"Make love to me, Hunter. Show me how much you love me."

Fire sparked and lit up within his eyes, his fingers tightened on her hips and he smiled. "With pleasure. But first," he pushed back off the bed and stood. Holding a hand out to her, he wiggled his fingers. "Come on, I have one more surprise for you."

"But—" She waved her hand out. "Show me later. Get back in this bed, mister."

His head fell back, his laughter echoing around the room. "Tsk, tsk, what a monster I've made. No, this surprise won't wait. And trust me, you'll want me to make love to you once you see it."

With a playful snarl, she slid from the bed and into his open arms.

His arms wrapped around her, nearly crushing her ribs as he devoured her mouth again.

Hands palming her ass, he lifted her, aligning her lace-covered pussy with his stiff shaft. She moved against him, desperate to have him inside her.

She nearly wept when he pulled back, breath rushing out of him. "Damn. Mmm, okay, let's go."

Hurrying after him, Andy roared with laughter, enjoying the morning. He made every day with him a new adventure.

Stopping short when he led her into the bathroom, she gasped. "Oh my God."

Dim light from the candles covering every surface cast an orange-yellow glow around the room. Rose petals littered the floor leading to the hot tub in the corner, and a vase of roses in all colors sat on the corner of the long vanity.

It was so romantic and touching, her heart melted. Tears pricked behind her eyes. He showed her in so many ways just how much he loved her.

She watched him turn on the faucets then he came back to her and lightly kissed her forehead. Looking down into her watery eyes, he smiled, and wiped away a tear with his thumb.

"Today is all for you, my love. I'm going to pamper you like you deserve and enjoy every minute with you."

"This is all too much. Dammit, Hunter." She sniffled. "You do so much for me. I don't deserve you."

He shook his head and smiled. "Nonsense. I love to please you."

Crouching, he pulled her panties down. He lifted one foot and then the other, and tossed the lacy undergarment into the corner.

His lips brushed over the bare flesh of her folds, his tongue sneaking out and lightly brushing her clit. With her hands tight in his hair, her head fell back as he made love to her center. She'd stand there forever if he just kept doing that.

"Mmm," he murmured when he pulled back. "Not just yet. Bath first."

She groaned but allowed him to lead her to the hot tub. Holding her hand, he helped her step in.

She leaned back. The heat of the water seeped into her bones, making her tingle.

"Hmm, this feels amazing." She gushed.

"I thought you might like it."

"Oh, yes. Definitely."

Andy looked up at him, and wiggled a finger at him, beckoning him closer. "Come here."

Propping himself on the side of the tub with his hands, he leaned over, bringing his face closer to hers. "What?" Their gazes connected.

She hoped he could see everything—the passion and the love she had for him.

"Thank you." She palmed the back of his head, pulling him in for a kiss.

Their tongues tangled and she heard him moan. She pulled back an inch and whispered, "I don't want to bathe alone."

He grinned down at her, stood and made quick work of getting out of his clothes. She threw her head back and laughed, feeling more carefree and at ease than she had in a long time.

He stepped into the tub and down onto his knees. His warm body slid along hers. Mischief and pleasure lit his eyes as he came closer.

When his mouth met hers, her last thought was that bathing alone was highly overrated.

Chapter Eight

"When do you think the remodel of the house will be finished, Andy?" Jeanine asked.

Hunter looked across the table at Andy. She never looked more beautiful than she did today. She'd been nervous cooking the meal for Thanksgiving, the first time they'd all sat down for a special occasion like this in ages. She'd put a lot of time into how she looked as well.

He'd been surprised when she'd mentioned inviting Tony and Jeanine for Thanksgiving, and even more shocked when she'd said she'd like to cook it at his place.

The house she had shared with Patrick was being remodeled room by room—except Peter's. Andy planned to leave it and remodel it herself when the rest was finished. She'd claimed she wanted a fresh start and since she hadn't felt comfortable spending any of Patrick's life insurance, there was more than enough to do so now.

Hunter was so proud of her.

In the six months they'd dated, she found herself again. Pride filled him that she'd done what she'd set out to do—push aside the guilt and live again.

"The contractor said it will be another couple of months. The master bedroom is the last room. I confess," she chuckled and looked at Jeanine, "I'll be glad to have some normalcy again. Waking up to the mess every day is getting old."

They all laughed.

Hunter kept the grin from spreading across his face, thinking about the mornings she hadn't woken up to the mess—nights she'd spent with him.

They hadn't hidden how much time they spent together—except for the evenings—from Tony or Jeanine. But out of respect, and because they were all still healing, they'd kept public displays of affection to a minimum.

Hunter gave his honorary parents a lot more credit, though.

Andy had fooled herself into thinking they weren't completely aware of their relationship since neither of them asked. But from the occasional glance from one or the other when he and Andy stood too close or shared a look of their own, Hunter was sure they'd caught on to how serious they were about each other by now. It was just like the older couple to not to pry into their lives, though.

"You could have stayed at our house, love," Tony reminded her.

Andy took a sip of her white wine then smiled. "I know, Dad. But I wanted to do this on my own. Everything has gone well." She gave his hand a pat. "If it gets too crazy in the next couple of months, I'll take you up on your offer."

Hunter smiled as their gazes connected. She wouldn't do that, but it was just like her to make Tony feel as if he could take care of her.

"So, Hunter, you've been awfully quiet. What's on your mind, son?" Jeanine questioned.

He looked at her, grabbed her hand and gently squeezed. His heart always warmed when she called him "son".

"Just sitting back after that great meal Andy slaved over. Great job, by the way." He winked at Andy, smiling when she blushed.

He found it funny that she could still blush after everything they'd done together in bed.

"Oh, yes, Andy. It was delicious, honey. Do you need help with dessert?" Jeanine offered.

"I thought we'd sit out on the balcony off Hunter's den and have our strawberry rhubarb..." Andy paused and looked at Tony. "...pie with whipped cream."

Tony scooted his chair back and let out a whoop. They all laughed as he gathered dishes and carried them to the sink. He was obviously in a hurry for some of his favorite dessert.

"Andy, you spoil him," Jeanine admonished, a wide smile on her face.

Tony wrapped his arms around Andy as she laid the dishes on the counter. "I love to be spoiled," he boasted and bussed Andy's cheek with a kiss.

Andy giggled. "You're incorrigible."

Hunter set the wineglasses on the counter and grabbed the white wine from the fridge. He refilled everyone's glass, his heart full at the noise filling his home. They should have done this before—his family at his place for a holiday meal. In years past, they always got together at the Sheavers or Patrick's. He vowed to make a point of having everyone over more often.

"She's a good daughter. Now, wife," Tony pulled Jeanine into his arms. "You spoil me on occasion, too, remember?" Tony waggled his eyebrows at her causing her to blush crimson.

Hunter nearly spit the wine he'd just taken a sip of back into his glass. He swallowed and turned to look at Andy.

She stood against the counter, her hands clasped in front of her, eyes watery. She met his gaze, shook her head, then turned to the counter and sliced into the pie.

Hunter glanced quickly at the lovebirds whispering to one another and sidled up beside her. "You okay, sweetheart?" he asked gently.

Andy nodded. "It's just so wonderful to see them happy."

He rubbed her shoulder. "They love how happy you are too, you know."

She looked up at him and grinned. "Thanks to you," she whispered.

Hunter wanted to lean down and kiss her. But until they'd told them, he'd wait. His gaze held hers, hoping she'd see the look of promise for later.

When she blushed and licked her lips, Hunter knew she understood.

She turned back to the plates on the counter, hands shaky. Hunter grabbed the silver serving tray from the counter and added the plates. He turned and chuckled at his parents.

"All right, you two. That's enough." He pushed open the kitchen door and held it open for his family. "Let's eat."

Tony laughed and slung an arm over Jeanine and Andy's shoulders. "Good idea."

Andy passed everyone a plate. Hunter relaxed in chair on one side of the table, and eyed the blue sky.

The evening was beginning to cool. The October weather was crisp but the evenings were still clear. He was glad the rain that had been almost a daily occurrence over the last week had stopped. Andy had hoped to have their dessert out on the balcony tonight.

He wasn't looking forward to the late November, early December snowfalls. He loved this time of year and wished winter never had to arrive. Maybe this year he and Andy could escape for a few weeks when the cold, snowy weather really descended on the city. Somewhere he could see her in a bikini every day and not a parka, scarf and mittens.

"Hunter," Andy demanded.

Pulled out of his decadent thoughts, he looked around the table. Three sets of gazes were on him. Andy and Jeanine looked concerned. Tony's look was sly as he smirked. Hunter felt the warmth in his cheeks at being the center of attention.

"Sorry, my mind wandered. I was appreciating the weather."

"Appreciating something all right," Tony said softly.

Hunter shook his head and pushed his fork into his pie. "Sorry, what were we discussing?"

"Andy was just telling me that she was hosting the Juvenile Diabetes Research Foundation event next week." Jeanine said. "I'm so thrilled."

Andy smiled and nodded. "I can't thank you enough for taking care of some of the fundraisers over the last year when I couldn't." She laid her hand over Jeanine's. "You have no idea how much that meant to me."

Jeanine squeezed her hand. "Nonsense, sweetie. That's what family is for."

"That's right, girlie," Tony cut in. "We're all family here. We'd do anything for you. And our boy here."

Hunter sent a smile his way. His heart clenched a bit, thinking about the two missing, cherished members who were rarely far from his thoughts.

Looking at Andy, his heart calmed and his mind pushed back the saddened thoughts. She was his saving grace. While she thought he'd saved her, she'd done exactly that for him too.

"Can we count on you to donate a nice lump sum to JDRF, Hunter?" Jeanine asked, unabashed as she took another bite of her pie.

Hunter laughed. His mom—that was how he thought of Jeanine—was nothing if not subtle, no matter how innocent she might look.

"Of course. I'll make sure it's the highest amount of the night." He winked.

She chuckled. "Good boy. I knew we'd be able to count on you."

"Always. I couldn't let Andy's first night back to hosting go without celebration. The amount will just be a bit larger than normal."

Andy slapped his arm. "Don't be silly. Any amount is appreciated. But thank you for the thought."

He'd do anything for her. Donate large sums of money, rub her feet, take out the trash—whatever it took to make her happy.

Tony cleared his throat and pulled Hunter's attention to him.

"You know, Hunter, Andy shouldn't go without a date for the evening. Maybe you should take our girl in order to keep all other men away from her. What do you think?"

"Tony!" Jeanine gasped.

"What? I'm just tossing the idea out there." Tony looked down at his plate, trying to appear innocent.

"Dad, you might be on to something," Andy commented.

They all focused on her.

Hunter's heart rate picked up speed when she sent an impish smile his way.

****

Andy looked at the three pairs of eyes staring at her.

Heat rose in her cheeks, and nerves settled into the pit of her stomach.

In preparing Thanksgiving this year, she'd also had an ulterior motive.

She wanted to tell her in-laws about her relationship with Hunter. While she'd needed the time to heal, she didn't like keeping such a thing from those she loved.

The last few months had proved to be challenging but complex to her future. She missed Patrick and Peter every day and she still worked through the pain of the loss and tragedy. Thanks to the weekly conversations with Mrs. Morrow—her new therapist—she understood that everything she once felt and her desire to move on were all natural and healthy. It was the next step in the healing process.

To honor the ones she loved was to remember the wonderful memories. Once her house was finished, she planned to put her favorite photos back up and not hide from the past.

There were a couple of her and Patrick she planned to hang in her office. While Hunter would understand and accept the love she'd had with her husband, she didn't want every picture in the main rooms to show it too much. Her living and sitting areas would still have pictures with Patrick, but only those with other family in them too.

And considering the question she wanted to pose to Hunter tonight, if he said yes, she wanted parts of the past to be resolved so they could begin a life together.

The future was always uncertain, but she couldn't imagine not being with him. He'd shown her that life could be wonderful after experiencing such tragedy. She fought hard against the grief and agony, and he'd shown her the way. Even after she'd given him every reason to walk away from her.

She looked at the faces around her and realized they waited for her to speak. She smiled and looked at Hunter. "It's a great idea. You should accompany me to the JDRF event."

Hunter blinked. Andy wanted to giggle at the priceless perplexed look on his face.

He constantly surprised her since they started dating, with flowers, weekend trips away, sexy lingerie and home cooked meals. She was thrilled to have finally caught him off guard for once.

Hunter cleared his throat and shifted in his chair. "Of course I'll take you. Not a problem."

"Good. Thank you." Andy winked. "Then there's the Breast Cancer Charity Auction at the end of the month. You should take me to that one too."

"Of course, that'll be fine."

Andy caught Tony's gaze across the table. He nodded encouragingly at her.

Her breath hitched. He knew what she was doing and had just given her his approval. She smiled back at him and tears filled her eyes. She took a deep breath and held herself together.

Perhaps she'd just been fooling herself, thinking they'd hidden their feelings for one another better.

"And isn't there an event in November?" Tony asked, feigned innocence all over his face. "The AIDS awareness one?"

Hunter's head moved back and forth from Tony to Andy, trying to keep up with the conversation.

She chuckled and looked at Tony. "Yes, you're right. Mom and I are both handling the whole thing this year. I definitely couldn't go without a date."

"There you go, sweetheart. You can't be going alone," Tony said.

Hunter stared at her. She hoped he understood that she knew exactly what she was doing, and ready to reveal the truth to the two people who loved them as much as they did one another. Weeks ago they'd discussed telling them everything but hadn't solidified it either. She hoped he understood her need to do it her way.

The light in his eyes sparkled as understanding dawned and he reached for her hand. She squeezed his tight and looked at Jeanine. The other woman, knowledge and happiness in her eyes, grabbed Andy's other hand. Jeanine's smile was huge and her watery eyes shone.

Yes, Andy realized she had been a fool all these months. She and Jeanine would have to sit down for a girl talk very soon.

"Well, I think it's time we headed home." Tony pushed his chair back and stood.

Surprised, Andy looked up at him. "Already?"

"Yep, give you two lovebirds time alone," he said.

Andy gasped as she watched him walk into the house. She stood and followed quickly. She needed to be sure he was okay with everything.

"Dad," Andy began as she walked into the kitchen. "Dad, are you okay?"

Tony stood in front of the counter, his palms flat and head bent. Andy laid a hand on his back when she stood beside him. He lifted his head and looked at her.

Andy's heart sank as tears shone in his eyes. But he smiled and chuckled. "I'm just fine, child. Don't worry about me."

He wiped his cheeks and took a deep breath. Andy leaned a hip against the counter, uncertain what to say. "Dad..."

He turned to face her and put both hands on her shoulders. "Now, don't worry. I'm happy for you and my boy out there."

"Then why the sadness?" Andy asked, hesitant.

"Sadness?" Tony scoffed. "No, sweetheart, I'm happy for you. You deserve another wonderful man in your life. I love Hunter as my own."

"I know you do."

"I do miss my other boys. But I'm thrilled for you." Tony swallowed hard. "Some days are difficult, but I look forward to seeing how you and Hunter grow together. You'll have been loved by two great men."

Andy smiled, teary-eyed. She wrapped her arms around his waist and laid her head on his shoulder. His arms enfolded her tight. "Nah, by three wonderful men, Dad. You'll always be my favorite."

Tony laughed loudly as she hoped he would. The sadness in the air lifted as she joined him and he squeezed her tight.

"Tony, is everything all right?" Jeanine asked softly when she walked into the kitchen.

Andy raised her head and caught Hunter's concerned gaze from where he stood in the doorway. She smiled wide to show him that all was okay.

"Of course, wife." Tony kissed the top of Andy's head, then walked toward Jeanine. "Let's head home. You gals can talk tomorrow."

Andy followed everyone out into the foyer. Hunter helped Jeanine with her light jacket, and kissed her cheek. By blood or not, he was such a dutiful and respectful son to them. And he knew just how to treat a lady. Andy's heart swelled with love and pride.

Tony bussed Andy's cheek again, and Andy hugged Jeanine. "I'll call you tomorrow, Mom."

Jeanine smiled wide and nodded. "You better, missy."

"Drive careful, Dad," Hunter ordered.

"Take care, son." Tony clutched Hunter's shoulder.

Andy looked away, tears returning when the two gave one another a tight hug.

Once she heard the door close, she turned. Hunter stood with his back to the door and his arms crossed over his chest.

Andy's body shivered at the bold and seductive look in his gorgeous eyes. She could have tears in hers one moment, and with just a look from him, she was ready to lie down and let him have his way with her—any way he wanted.

She smiled and walked into the living room. She sat on the floor, on the lush carpet in front of the fireplace.

"You know you surprised the hell out of me tonight, don't you?" Hunter asked as he came over to the where she sat and lowered himself behind her, his legs on both sides of her.

He kissed her neck and moaned low when her body shivered. He knew the exact effect he had on her. Andy could hide nothing of her body's response from him.

She leaned her head against the side of his arm to give him greater access to her. "Mmm, why do you say that?"

Hunter nibbled her earlobe, then said, "I wasn't expecting you to tell them about us. We hadn't really decided on it to be tonight."

Andy shifted and looked at him. She frowned. "Are you upset? I'm sorry—"

"No, no." Hunter lightly kissed her lips. "Not at all. I'm relieved."

She snuggled into his arms and looked at the fireplace. "Me too. We should have done it sooner."

"Was Dad really okay?"

Andy smiled, her heart full at the memory of her father-in-law giving her his blessing, and his love. "Yes, more than okay. He really loves you."

His arms tightened around her. "I know."

They sat in silence, both looking into the fire.

Andy had definitely been blessed. She had found love twice in her lifetime and would hold on to it with everything she had. There were always unexpected moments in life, tragedies of loss and pain, but she would make every moment seem like the last.

She no longer wanted the tortured pain of rough sex that she once thought she needed. Nor did she believe she deserved whatever horrible thing might happen to her. To honor those she loved, she needed to live. Really live. With love, laughter and everything that was important to her.

Peter and Patrick were forever in her heart and soul. Nothing would ever replace either of them, but she had found new love, a life that held so many possibilities.

Hunter saved her. From herself and the agony.

Her love for him went so deep; she never wanted to face life without him.

Andy tipped her head back and met his gaze. Love shone bright in his eyes and warmed her entire body. She would treasure his love every day.

She laid a hand on his cheek. Drawing his face down to hers, she captured his lips. Soft and lazy, their lips moved against one another. Love and desire circled through her.

Andy pulled back and smiled. "I love you," she admitted for the first time.

Hunter drew in a deep breath then grinned. "I love you, too."

Heart full, Andy couldn't believe how happy she was. She looked at the fire, then back at Hunter again. "When the house is finished, I think you should move in with me."

Hunter's eyes widened, then a huge smile spread across his face. "I think that's a fantastic idea."

"Good." Andy smiled. "I'm glad you agreed since I'm having an additional office added."

Hunter chuckled. "Sure of yourself, weren't you?"

Andy shook her head and ran a finger over his lips. "No. Just sure of us."

He lowered his head and captured her mouth once more.

Andy poured every ounce of love and hunger into the kiss. She savored the taste of the man in her arms, and the future that awaited them.

The End

DEDICATION

To all my readers who wanted to see more of these characters and learn more about the Club. Who am I to say no to any of you? Enjoy!

CLUB SPLENDOR: VOLUME ONE

SWEETEST SPLENDOR

Club Splendor, 2

Kacey Hammell

Copyright © 2013

Chapter One

"You'll be missed around here. I expect to see you soon." Bridget Guthrie's boss gave her a tight hug, and she reciprocated his embrace.

"I'll definitely stop by as often as I can. Give Andy my best, too." She exited his office, closed the door behind her and hurried down the dimly lit hallway, trying to hold her tears at bay.

She'd loved her job every day of the last five years. As hostess at Club Splendor for three of those years, she'd connected with a lot of people, built relationships with the staff and anticipated coming to work every day. One of the hottest spots in Ottawa, the club maintained a full membership and requests poured in consistently. No other job rewarded her as much as this one had.

But Bridget had dreams she wanted to pursue. Tonight was her last night here and new beginnings started tomorrow.

Grabbing the clipboard from the bar, she headed into the private areas of the club. All hallways were dimly lit, each room decorated with rich, sensuous black and burgundy, golds and reds. Corner booths took up most of the bar area, as well as within private viewing areas that were curtained off and secluded to afford privacy.

Only personally invited people became members at Splendor. Hunter Sullivan was selective in his clientele—most were friends and acquaintances of other participants, all of whom underwent extreme background checks, meetings and extra-personal questions about their sex lives. And he expected the absolute strictest confidence from all his staff.

Bridget intended to become a member someday. Perhaps now she'd have that chance since she'd no longer be working here come Monday. Hunter had such strict rules about his employees being members, or becoming involved with any of the current ones, that leaving meant she'd finally be free to explore the more titillating side of Club Splendor. She wanted to give herself the chance to indulge some deep-seated sexual fantasies, like being a part of a trio, being watched … to see how far her darkest desires truly went.

She checked room after room, making sure they were no longer occupied. Though she'd been hired as hostess, Hunter also gave her some managerial duties. She prided herself on giving members everything they needed, and had everything at their disposal from the beginning of their arrival to the very end. Now, she anticipated their needs and worked hard to ensure perfection in everything. Many of them called her personally if they requested something new, or to arrange kinkier games to try, or a specific group dalliance they'd never participated in before.

Bridget closed the second last door and crossed the hall to the last room.

Her favorite.

The plush black carpeting, the red leather sofas and chaise, and the cinnamon scent filled her senses with decadence and comfort. Red curtains hid clear glass, allowing an audience to watch. Each room connected to viewing areas where other members engaged in whatever carnal acts they chose.

Clientele understood they might be watched at any moment, and all signed off on it. The club's strict rules of keeping identities and names secret allowed everyone the safety and privacy they sought, since many people might frown upon what happened behind closed doors. Members who enjoyed the kinkier, decadent and sometimes D/s lifestyles paid a lot of money for the safety and trust of the owner and staff.

She scanned her clipboard to discover the names of the people on the other side of the glass. Seeing Paige & Nolan's names on the paper, her heart skipped a beat. They were one of her favorite married couples to deal with. Pleasant, fun, and spontaneous, and neither were shy when it came to sex. They made her job very easy.

Bridget had even come to know Paige a bit outside of the club. They'd met for lunch a few times and found they had a lot in common. She'd been one of the first to encourage Bridget to reach for her big career dream.

She found Paige a stunning and erotic woman with a charming, attentive sexual tiger for a husband – the kind of man Bridget longed to find. And she hoped to dig deep enough and find great sexuality in herself, like Paige had. Confident, sexy, uninhibited…

Bridget heaved a sigh and sat on the sofa, crossing off the completed tasks from her to-do list. She had so many desires and fantasies, but no vast experience with sex.

Twenty-nine years old, and most of her experiences came from watching others in the back rooms of the club if she happened to catch a peek while checking on clients. The three men she'd been involved with weren't ones she'd ever brag about. All were selfish, quick, and uncaring about her needs.

As much as she longed to be a member of Club Splendor, she wouldn't be talking to Hunter about it any time soon. Nervous butterflies fluttered in her stomach just thinking about it.

The door swung open, startling her. Recognizing the man who entered, she smiled. "Zander, what are you doing here?"

Zander Hudson was the perfect specimen of manhood. Clichéd, but tall, dark and handsome fit him exactly. His curly and black hair reached the nape of his neck, well-kept but unruly. Her fingers itched often to run through it to see if it was as silky as it seemed.

She considered his hunter-green eyes deep recesses of knowledge and kindness. He listened whenever someone spoke to him, and he always focused on whomever he spoke with. He'd started as a maître d' but had since been promoted to Assistant Manager. They'd become friends working together over the last three years, and she confided in him a lot.

They'd also flirted, shared a few caresses and lingering touches. She enjoyed the long and smoky glances he sent her way when he thought she wasn't looking. But the club's strict *no staff fraternization* rule kept them from acting on their mutual attraction.

He shoved the door behind him and leaned against it, arms crossed over his chest, a scowl on his face. "I leave for two weeks and find out from the new bartender that you're leaving."

So he was unhappy with her career change. Bridget let out a breath, and set the clipboard on the seat beside her. God, he was sexy and fine standing there, dressed in all black, his shirt unbuttoned--probably because of the humid summer weather--and showing off the tan he'd gotten while in Miami. "I'm sorry. I tried to reach you before you left, but I wasn't able to."

He gaped at her. "You haven't heard of texting?"

"I wasn't about to bother you on vacation. I planned to come see you tomorrow." She frowned. "Why are you home a day early?"

"That's not important." He pushed away from the door and took a seat next to her. "You're really leaving."

He hadn't posed it as a question but she nodded anyway. Zander grabbed her hand and held it between both of his. "You're the captain that really runs this place, you know."

She laid her head on his shoulder, comfortable in their friendship. But her heart raced, reminding her that she wished they could be more.

If only she had the courage to share how she really felt about him…no, she wasn't going there. Now was not the time. There'd be little to no time for a new relationship once she started school. Striving for a double business degree, which involved double the classes and workload, wouldn't leave much time for anything else. She wished she could keep her job here and do it all, but it would be too much of a burden, and something had to give.

"Carleton University, huh," Zander grumbled, shoving his shoulder against hers.

"Yeah, double business. I'm planning to be done in two years instead of four. That's why I needed to quit, to be finished sooner."

He laced his fingers in hers. His touch sent sparks along her arm. If only he knew what he did to her. How her pussy quivered being this close to him. She took a deep breath, lifted her head from his shoulder and scooted away. "I have to get a few more things done before I call it a night."

"Everything finalized with Hunter? You know Andy's going to miss you."

Bridget smiled. Andy, their boss' fiancée, was another person she'd grown close to in the last year. They'd known one another for about four years, but since Andy started seeing Hunter and came around more, she and Bridget had become good friends, too.

Years ago, Andy had frequented the club with Patrick, her then-husband, but after his death, she and Hunter had finally realized their romantic feelings for one another. Bridget had adored Patrick, even harboured a bit of a crush on him, and was saddened by his untimely death. He'd always been such a gentleman with her, sharing humorous stories, and flirting a little. Bridget missed him very much.

She shook those sad memories from her mind. "It's not as though I'll never stop around to say hi, you know. I'll miss seeing everyone all the time, but this is important to me." She stood and walked to the table beside the stairs that led into the other mirrored hideaway. Members solely watched the events in the other room or were welcomed to join in, but all participants had to be in agreement.

Remembering the couple on the other side of the curtain, a shiver snaked along her spine. If alone, and since Paige and Nolan were probably the last couple in the building, Bridget might have considered taking a peek.

It was one of her favorite aspects of each room. A simple push of the button and all participants became aware of each other if they wished, since the glass could be controlled as one-sided or not. It wouldn't be the first time she'd watched Paige and Nolan in secret. But she'd never had the guts to change the settings to let them see her too.

"I know following your dreams is important to you, Bridget. I'm happy for you." Zander sidled closer, and massaged her stiff shoulders.

"Thank you. I know you are. It's just—" she swallowed past the lump in her throat. "It is hard to think of leaving. I love this job. I'll miss it."

"You'll miss me more though, right?" His light tone lifted her mood.

She laughed. "Of course. Who else will I get to boss around?"

He chuckled and pulled her in to his chest, aligning her against his stomach. Her breath hitched as his arms wrapped around her waist and squeezed her tight. Her nipples tingled and her heart rate accelerated.

Being this close to him, his long body behind her, the dreams she had about a moment like this…. She wished she could turn in his arms, press her lips to his and see where it led. But their friendship meant a lot to her. The fun flirting and teasing had never gone to the next level, but no other man in her life affected her more.

And now they would no longer be working together…but she wasn't sure how deep his feelings for her ran.

"Damn, you smell good. What is that you're wearing?" Zander asked, his face buried in her neck.

"Umm, something berry I guess." Her words sounded breathless even to her own ears. He never held her like this before. She shivered.

"You cold?" He ran his palms over her stomach, then his arms tightened around her.

She shook her head, speechless, about to melt into a puddle at his feet. Relaxing into his embrace, she aligned with his front. "Zander--"

"You know I've always wondered something about you," he murmured.

"What's that?" she questioned, mouth dry.

"If any of what happens around this place excites you," he whispered against her neck.

She reclined her head on his shoulder, sighing. Could she confess her innermost thoughts to him?

The air in the room heightened at least twenty degrees. The fire in her belly spread along her limbs to her fingertips. "Why is that important to you?"

Clasping her hands in his, he rasped, "I've always had the desire to know what makes you tick. I've watched you a long time, secretly wanting to know more about you. Finding reasons to be close to you."

Excitement slithered along her body, her heart nearly leaping from her chest.

"We've been friends a long time, Bridget, but you know what? I want more." He ran his lips along her neck, warming her skin until they reached her ear. "Tell me what turns you on," he whispered, then captured her earlobe in his teeth.

Chapter Two

Bridget gasped and inched away from him. Turning, her eyes locked with his. Her bottom came up against the table behind, her heart racing, realizing there was little room to move. She was trapped. Nerves skated down her spine. The hunger and need in the darkness of his eyes emboldened her, filling her with a confidence she never experienced before.

No time to think about that. Not when desperate need coursed through her. His first kiss against her skin changed things. There was no way she'd accept just friendship with him now.

Anxious, wanting to hold onto this moment with him, and share her innermost desires, she grabbed the remote from the table and hit a button. The curtains behind her opened. She watched Zander's eyes shift upward and go wide. They returned to hers and he grinned.

Bridget hit another button and the room filled with moans and sounds of flesh slapping against flesh. She trembled hearing the couple's rough, but no doubt exhilarating, sex behind the glass. Always hard on each other while at the same time as gentle as their love, both enjoyed vigorous and no-holds barred sex and gave no apologies.

Zander stepped toward her, and skimmed his palms across her stomach, creating heat and butterflies circling inside her. So hot. His skin warmed her.

But when he lowered his head to hers, his lips gliding against hers, all thoughts fled and she pulled him closer, need and anticipation filling her.

Empowered, she slipped her tongue inside of his mouth. He moaned and opened wider for her, allowing her to discover the delicious taste of him. Cupping his ass cheeks, she held him close as they explored, and his palms drifted over the globes of her bottom.

Her heart thrummed as he fisted the soft cotton of her skirt then tugged her even closer. She didn't think it was possible to be so absorbed in this man. She craved crawling all over him for endless hours.

Zander pressed his forehead against hers. "Bridget," he muttered, "I want you. So much."

"I want you too." She brushed her lips against his.

Lifting his hands, he made quick work of the buttons of her blouse. He pulled open the sides, and groaned. "This is what you wear to work?"

He smoothed his fingers along the valley between her breasts and skimmed over the sheer see-through material of her bra. She loved lingerie and spent as much money as possible at Victoria's Secret. Her one indulgence, she treated to herself whenever she socked her school money away from her allotted bi-weekly checks or any extra income from working more hours at the club.

His wide and hungry eyes made her feel sexy and she smirked at him. "You don't like it?"

"If I liked it any better I'd have a heart attack right now. Jesus, gorgeous…your tits are so hot behind that lacy stuff."

She giggled. "The panties match."

He sucked in a deep breath, turned her around and clasped the zipper, then eased it down.

Bridget's eyes lifted to the glass. "Oh my God," she gasped.

Both naked on the bed, Paige's fingers held Nolan's head between her thighs. His tongue flicked in rapid succession, his lips feasting on his wife's pussy.

"Like that, do you, babe?" Zander questioned, and pushed her skirt to the floor. His palms cupped her bottom. "I love it. Fucking love your choice of underwear, too. Your tight ass is spectacular. I could stare at you all day."

Bridget pulled her gaze from the couple then glanced over her shoulder at him. "That's all you want to do, look?"

His eyes narrowed on her. "Hell, no. Turn around. You can watch your peep show another time, but I want to see that pussy of yours."

She turned toward him on the short heels, hands on her hips and let his gaze wander over her body, trying not to fidget. Never had she stood before a man like this – allowing him to see all her flaws. She was far from a size two – or hell, even a twelve – but she tried to watch what she ate and took care of herself. Unfortunately, the late hours she worked didn't allow for the best eating habits. There were curves in places she wished there weren't but wouldn't call herself overweight.

"Spread your legs for me," Zander commanded in a gruff tone. Excitement shot down her spine. Complying, she widened her stance.

"I can see your wetness from here. It's sexy as hell." His gaze lifted, spearing her with a look of smoldering intensity and direct and open honesty. "I want you."

Bridget swallowed hard. She needed to be consumed by him and taken with everything he had to give her. "And our friendship?"

He shook his head. "We've already crossed the line. I won't settle for less now. You mean too much to me. *This* means too much to me."

She grinned and cocked her hip. Lowering one hand, she skimmed her fingers over the front of her panties. Zander's jaw clenched, spellbound by her ministrations. "Neither will I. Can you handle it?"

"Fuck, yeah, I can." He grabbed the remote and closed the curtain then shut off the volume. "Another time we might ask to join them. Tonight, I want you all to myself." He reached for her.

Swooping low, he caught her mouth with his. Passion swirled around them. Moans filled the room. Raising his head, deep breathing the only sound around them, he laid his forehead against hers. "Your taste makes my dick hard and my heart pound, baby."

"Zander," she moaned and shoved the shirt off his shoulders. Her gaze locked on his as her hands explored his skin, gliding over the ridges and glorious muscles. Hard, manly and sexy, she'd be happy to touch him like this for days and never grow tired of it.

Undoing her bra, she dropped it to the floor, then inched her fingers over his nipples. He groaned. Tweaking and pinching each bud, she smiled when he surrendered to her touch. Bridget leaned in, her tongue swept one pebble then the other, and she inhaled deep. His woodsy and masculine scent filled her. She trembled.

She bit at his nipple, nipping the swollen peak. The heady taste of body wash mixed with sweat tasted so good to her, she hoped every part of him had the same unique flavour. Wanting to have her fill of his taste, she rained kisses along his chest, her lips and tongue taking turns as they moved along his neck.

Fingers digging into her long hair, he hauled her in closer, his breathing deep. "You taste so good," she whispered in his ear, and bit his lobe between her teeth.

She grinned, revelling in this man in her arms, making him groan and quake. A euphoria of confidence raced through her. No man had ever surrendered to her like this. Allowed her control and setting the pace. It was splendid and intoxicating.

Dragging her lips over his shoulder, she worked her way down his chest. His hold on her head tightened as she grasped the button of his jeans, and opened his zipper.

"Bridget," he growled, his tone husky with warning.

"I know, I know. You taste so good," she mumbled between kisses. "I want to taste all of you."

Falling to her knees, she watched him as she lowered his jeans and his hard shaft bobbed out. She purred at the delicacy in front of her, the length and girth so splendid, she couldn't wait to have him inside her. Fisting his cock, Bridget leaned in and flicked the head with her tongue. Zander hissed through his teeth.

"I can't wait to suck on this." Her palms cupped his cock, caressed his stomach, and savoured the hardness under her fingers. Such a glorious sight he was.

"I don't know if I'll be able to hold back with your mouth around me," he muttered, his fingers tangling in her hair.

Bridget grinned, knowing he wasn't going to stop her from finding out. Cupping his balls in one hand and his shaft in the other, she took the long flesh in, her jaw relaxing as it worked over him.

Taking a deep breath, she inhaled and took all of him. He gasped above her, his arms falling to his sides, fists clenched.

She eased back, and then quickly took all of him in again. Over and over, she sucked his flesh deep, relishing in the warm, silky taste of him. She nibbled along the length of his shaft as she fondled his sac. She couldn't get enough of him. He was everything she'd always dreamed of.

Lifting her eyes upward, she found him watching her, his gaze locked on his shaft sliding in and out of her mouth. Potent lust, dark and rich, flared in the depths. Bridget didn't know how she'd waited so long to experience such a pure and exhilarating moment like this with him.

Palms cupped her cheeks, his light touch caressing as they hollowed and she sucked him deep, tracing her lips around his cock as she sucked. He rocked his hips, feeding his dick to her. Bridget held herself immobile, her hands on his hips, as he glided in and out of her. He seemed in awe of her, gaze locked on her mouth as he fucked it.

"You're so damn hot on your knees. Mouth perfectly rounded as I stuff my dick in you," Zander rumbled, his fist tight on her jaw. She squeezed his hips, forcing him to move faster. Eyes flaring, her fervor blazed hotter as he moved faster.

She moaned, exhilarated in this sense of abandon and the complete sexiness of this moment. Giddy and elated, her inner seductress loved it. Zander brought out so much empowerment and luscious emotions from her.

Opening her mouth wider, he pumped inside her steadily and with ease. He growled and clasped her shoulders. His dick fell from her lips as he pulled her to her feet. Claiming her lips with his own, he feasted on her, growling low when her fingers surrounded and pumped him hard.

Walking her backward, he pulled hard, tearing the underwear from her. Bridget gasped, shocked, excitement building inside. She back-pedaled until her calves hit something solid, and sat. His lips left hers as he positioned her on the red chaise lounge.

She always wondered what it would be like to have sex on a piece of furniture like this. Curved and soft, it cupped her body and leveraged her hips at the perfect height for where he stood. The washable microfiber moulded her body, cradling her in comfort and relaxation.

Zander gazed at her, hungry and devouring, as he pushed her legs back. Spread out in front of him, Bridget sucked in a deep breath. He licked his lips, jaw clenching as he stepped out of his jeans.

She'd never seen him so ferocious or sexy. This was a man who wanted to claim his woman and she didn't think she'd be walking out of the room any time soon. She had no argument for it, as she planned to spend as much time worshipping him as possible.

"I love these new lounging things Hunter brought in," Zander said. "I've heard many of the members discussing how much they love them, and the new positions they've found." He skated his palms along the inside of her spread thighs, teasing her as they moved up and down, closer and closer to her pussy but never touching.

"I look forward to trying out all the positions imaginable with you." He leaned over the high end and blew on her open flesh.

Bridget's head fell back on the cushion and her breath escaped in a rush. Ticklish and spectacular, the air over her swollen and wet flesh sent a shiver along her spine. Her feet flattened more firmly on the seat, her thighs falling open even further, eager for more.

Zander chuckled then blew again. She lifted her hips, anxious for more. So thrilling, while agony at the same time. "Zander," she purred. Raising her arms, she gripped the chaise on either side of her head. "Please," she murmured.

"Please what, babe?" He blew again. "Doesn't that feel good?"

Her juices flowed as the cool air surrounded her flesh. "It's so good. Amazing. But I want you inside me." She breathed deep, her clit swelling and inner muscles throbbing. If he didn't get inside her soon, she'd have to take control back. Arching her back, her nipples beaded as images of him plunging deep, hard and fast played in her mind.

"Zander," she whined, gripping her thighs. She glared at him. "Take me."

He grinned and moved to the side, angling himself between her thighs. He winked at her then lowered his head. His lips swept along her pussy, and sucked her clit. Bridget shrieked, delight and electricity coursing through her.

Elevating her head, she watched Zander love her pussy, leaving no inch untouched. Moist and warm, he had a spectacular technique that she hoped to take advantage of many times over. But she needed him inside her, plunging deep and helping her reach perfect ecstasy.

His lips surrounded her clit, pulled the nub into his mouth, teeth pinching and teasing. Pleasure washed through her, consuming her. She pulled her legs back, palms holding her thighs higher, bringing her closer to his mouth. He consumed her, licking and slurping her juices. Ecstasy and torture. She needed him so much.

Zander pulled back. She watched him close his eyes and lick his lips. Opening his eyes, he gazed at her open thighs and hummed. Her heart skipped beats, loving the fact that he seemed so absorbed in her, his face an open book of awe, sensuality and warmth.

"So pretty," he crooned. He pushed two fingers into his mouth, wetting them, then withdrew them and rubbed along her clit. Her back bowed. An inferno spread in the wake of his touch. She gasped.

"I can't wait to fuck you. You want to be filled here, don't you?" He punctuated his statement by shoving his fingers inside her. A shriek escaped, her chest heaving as she tried to breathe.

"Ahh, damn, babe. You're so full. So swollen and aching to come. Damn, my dick's so hard." He thrust his fingers inside, pumping them in and out, burying them in to the hilt and caressing her g-spot.

Her palms fell from her thighs and clenched the fabric of the chaise. Such vivid and unadulterated pleasure. Nothing had ever come close to this. No man ever made her bones melt or her body vibrate with so much energy before. She never wanted it to end, while at the same time, she desperately needed it to end. And she'd be anxious to do it all over again.

She groaned as Zander's fingers fell from her body and he stood. His fist wrapped around his shaft, his gaze dark and worshipping her as it flickered over her body. Tears pricked at the back of her eyes. Such passion in his gaze … no one had ever looked at her like that before.

Raising her arms, she beckoned, "Make love to me." The hard and furious need inside her craved no-holds-barred sex. But watching him, seeing the truth of his emotions in his eyes, she knew she would be making love to this man. She had to be honest with herself: her life would be forever changed today. She'd dreamed about this for a long time and would never be able to get enough.

Bridget shifted higher on the seat, allowing him to move in between her thighs. She sent a thank you to the creative gods for inventing such a magnificent piece of furniture that put them close together and angled perfectly for comfort and ease. The many positions they could enjoy that came to mind were endless. And she'd be willing to try out every single one.

"Your body is a piece of art," Zander murmured as he pulled a foil packet from his jeans. He opened the foil, and rolled protection over his shaft.

She didn't want anything between them. Right now, she needed him.

Humbled, she reached out and stroked his cheek. "Yours is pretty fantastic too."

He smiled then eased the tip of his cock at her opening. "It'd kill me, but ... you're sure about this?"

Bridget nodded, awed by his consideration and understood that he would stop if she wished. Where had this man come from? She was one lucky woman.

"More certain about this than anything else. I want you."

Chapter Three

Excitement washed through Bridget as Zander eased inside her. Her channel walls burned and tingled as he eased in. The width of him spread her wider than she'd ever been.

"Damn, you're tight. Fucking perfect," he snarled through clenched teeth. Sparks ignited through her body seeing him as immersed in this as she was.

With his hands under her knees, holding her legs back, Bridget felt every bit of friction from his cock. She relaxed her vaginal muscles, allowing him to push even further, and bury himself deeper inside her. Her loud groan mingled with his.

Her eyes never left him as he eased away then shoved inside her again. Their gazes locked as he claimed her and made slow love to her.

On fire and consumed with the man before her, Bridget lifted her hands and clasped her breasts. Having Zander inside her was so good. Her mind closed to everything but the two of them and the sounds of sex and the light odour of sweat around them.

Pinching her nipples, the sparks of excitement travelled through her, making her insides quiver. She grinned as the walls of her channel tightened around his cock. His head fell back, a moan pulled from him.

Tweaking and playing on the swollen peaks, decadence coursed through her, sweeping her away. Relaxing, she let herself go. His focus on her, the passion he shared with her and the way he gazed at her, made her confident and uninhibited.

"Yeah, touch yourself. You're so hot like this, laid open for me, touching yourself."

She purred, delight snaking through her. "I love your dick inside me, filling me, making my pussy weep. You're so hard," she cried out as he plunged deep.

His eyes lit up, as green as woods overflowing with trees. "Tell me more," he growled, thrusting steady and harder.

Bridget smirked, pleased that he enjoyed vocal sex. She loved listening to the club members' moans and gasps of ecstasy through the speakers whenever she had the chance. "My body's blazing hot. Nipples are so hard. Mmm, yes, fuck me. Hard."

He moaned, picking up speed. Joy washed through her.

"Faster. Please, Zander. I want you. So much," she begged, not above expressing her need.

A shriek escaped her as his hands cupped her ass, lifting her higher, and freeing him to move faster. He cantered strong and powerful, his dick pounding her wet pussy, hard and rough.

"Yes. Oh my God, yes. That's it. More," Bridget cried, her arms gripping the end of the chaise. She lifted her hips, welcoming him.

Their slick bodies moved in harmony, their gasps filling the room. Lost in the tumultuous and exquisite delight taking over her, she savoured him inside her.

"I've never loved fucking someone so much in my life. You were made for my dick. So sweet, so wet and those muscles hold me so tight," Zander whispered, joy in his eyes.

"Zander," she sighed, fists clenched, her body bowed. "God."

"I know, babe, I know." He shifted higher onto his knees, seating deeper inside. He touched every nerve within her walls, hitting her g-spot so powerfully, she considered staying there forever.

Release rushed toward her. Her fingers tingled and her nipples tightened. Her juices flowed and eased from her.

"Fuck, you're so wet. Damn. I can't wait for you to spray all over my dick," Zander snarled, thrusting harder.

His words catapulted her off the edge. A scream tore through Bridget as she fell, ecstasy tearing from her, pulling her into darkness.

From far away she heard an agonized shout, as the warmth of his cum filled her. Another orgasm tore through her. The world spun, leaving her with no center of gravity and light headed.

When it seemed like pins poked her skin, Bridget returned to earth and her eyes opened, her body relaxed and languid. Breathing heavy, she peeked at Zander, his torso brushing hers as he held himself on his arms above her. She wrapped her arms around his shoulders, pulling him on top of her, cradling him against her body.

His heavy gusts of breath matched hers and warmed her neck as he rested.

Her palms massaged over his moist back, captivated with the contour of muscle beneath. His now flaccid penis began to slide from her, the cooling wetness of their mixed juices making her shiver.

Zander's head lifted, peering at her, his eyes a warm green. His face relaxed, the lines of his mouth shifted into a smile.

He leaned down, his lips brushing hers, and relaxed on his elbows positioned on each side of her head. "Hey there," he muttered.

Bridget almost laughed at the casual comment but was too relaxed. She giggled. "Hey back. And here I thought there might be a bit of awkwardness."

He shook his head, his fingers tracing her cheek. "Nah. We've been friends too long. Hell, I've come onto you more times than I ever have with any woman. Usually once not reciprocated, I don't like to be a pest about it," he grinned.

She rolled her eyes, arms wrapped around his back, comfortable and content. "It's not like I didn't flirt back. We're sticklers for morals and all that I guess."

He chuckled. "Maybe. But Hunter's been there for both of us. Who are we to break his rules now that you're no longer employed here?" He kissed her nose. "I plan to make up for lost time. Every possible second of every single day that I can."

Happy, she laughed out loud. He lowered, his mouth meeting hers, swallowing the last of her humour as his tongue swept in. Her body smoldered all over again.

Bridget panted, spirals of arousal filtering through her. Oh, how he got the bonfire inside her from zero to eighty degrees so fast.

He laid his forehead against hers. "What you do to me."

"I can say the same. You know, we're probably the last two here."

Zander lifted his head. "Probably. But we've been the last two to leave many times before."

She shrugged. "Sure, but not like this."

His fingers trailed along her arm. "Are you complaining?"

"Not at all, but maybe we should go to my place? Continue this there?"

He smirked. "I say we stay right here. We're closed tomorrow. The cleaning crew will be in later than normal tomorrow because of a staff shortage, right? We have the rest of the night to ourselves." His gaze swept the room. "I'd imagine we can find lots to occupy us in here."

Bridget smiled, liking his train of thought. The room was by far the most, well-stocked place for adult toys and titillating choices of erotic play than anywhere she'd ever heard of.

"Sounds naughty and decadent," she murmured, her fingers sliding over his spine and tightening in his unruly hair.

His teeth nipped her shoulder. "One night will never be enough with you. I hope you know I want more than just tonight."

Her heart pounded, and adrenaline rushed through her at his words and his hot mouth sliding across her neck. His hardening bulge rubbed against her pussy. "No," she agreed. "One night won't be enough. I'll need many, many nights like this before I'm through with you."

He latched his lips around her right breast. She arched off the lounge, his mouth hollowing out as he suckled her. Her pussy rekindled hot and her hold on him tightened.

Awash in gratification, her hand shifted between them and fisted around his hard-on. He groaned around the bounty in his mouth, and her fingers squeezed.

Zander shifted back. "You know what I've always dreamed of doing to you?" he questioned, rolling his shaft in her grasp.

Thrilled he had thought of the two of them together like this, she had to know. "What's that?" She stroked him from base to tip. Her other hand cupped and fondled his sac. He fit her hands so perfectly, as if he belonged there.

His eyes locked on hers as his breath quickened. "I want to take your ass," he admitted, tone hushed and soft.

Bridget's eyes widened and her ministrations on his dick ceased.

Chapter Four

Only once before had she trusted a man enough to let him take her from behind… Such an intimate act between lovers, at least to her. But that former lover had made it horrible for her. No finesse, no ease and no care for the pain he'd bestowed on her.

"Too soon?" Zander pulled her between his legs and laid each of hers over his.

"Umm," she began.

"Hey, no worries. It's too much too soon. I understand it's not to everyone's tastes." He clasped onto her hands and pulled her up. He wrapped his arms around her, cradling her against him.

"No. No, it's not that. I…I would love to experience everything with you," she whispered, fingers caressing his arms. "The one and only time I did it, was not the best experience of my life."

His hold tightened on her and his jaw clenched. "Tell me about it?" he asked, gruff and hard.

Her heart jumped knowing he was pissed off on her behalf. She ran a finger over his lips. "Not a lot to tell. It hurt like hell. He didn't give me time to adjust, and sure as hell didn't care about my pleasure."

"Son-of-a-bitch. I'm sorry."

"Not your fault. But it has soured me about it."

Zander pulled her in close, rubbing her back.

Moisture filled her eyes. This man was so wonderful, so caring. She knew he would never do anything to hurt her.

Nerves untangled around her heart as she weakened to the possibility of trusting him enough to shatter the horrific memories of the past. He'd take care of her.

"I'm sorry it happened to you. No guy should ever treat a woman like that. Give me his name, I'll track him down."

Bridget laughed and eased back. "My He-Man. Thank you, but he's long gone."

"You deserve better."

She swallowed hard. The openness in his gaze, the protectiveness – in his words and the way he held her – denying him anything was impossible. "You'll do it better, right?"

His green eyes darkened with heat. He inhaled hard. "You're a fucking princess. You deserve soft hands, kindness and patience. But you don't have to decide tonight."

Smiling at him, she nodded. "I know. It's my choice. But…." Her gaze swept the room and landed on the cherry oak cabinet in the corner. Glass and rubber dildos of every shape and size enclosed inside. All new and part of the package that each member received, the cabinet looked full to capacity, which meant they'd have a wide variety of toys to choose from.

"But?" Zander interrupted her thoughts.

"Will you fuck me with one of those," she tilted her head toward the corner, "while you fill my ass?"

His fingers flexed as his gaze shifted. His nostrils flared and his dick bumped against her thigh. "I guess you like the idea?"

"Fucking. Love. It."

He kissed her, hard. "Are you sure?"

She nodded and untangled herself from his lap. After pulling him to his feet, she pointed to the cabinet. "Get what you need."

Bridget kneeled on the chaise and ogled the tight posterior of the man she couldn't wait to have inside her again. Toned, tanned and splendid, his cheeks were made to hold on to.

He opened the cabinet and inspected the items. He hummed as he pondered, nearly making Bridget laugh aloud, then pulled something from within. She tried to peek around him but in his position, she was unable to see anything. A shiver of anticipation raced through her at the possibilities.

Rifling in a drawer at the bottom of the cabinet, he withdrew a cloth and a tube of lubrication. Bridget's mouth dried, nerves skating along her limbs. She drew in a deep, calming breath.

Zander pivoted then stalked toward her.

At least eight inches long, in clear glass and a handhold on the end, her eyes widened as she caught sight of the object in his hand. She gulped but her pussy quivered. She licked her lips, imagining what the wide spiralled texture would feel like inside her.

Anticipation filled her, and her heart fluttering, she shifted onto her knees and leaned on the end of the chaise.

Zander approached her, his shaft bobbed eagerly. "Looks like I made the right choice," he smiled, and brought his hand down on her with a playful spank. "You have no idea how many nights I got off, thinking of you like this. Bent over, ready for my cock, waiting to be fucked."

Bridget trembled and shifted, her nipples rubbing against the microfiber. She gasped, stunned and she moved again. Flames erupted in her pussy. She spread her knees apart further, letting the cool air waft over the heat.

"Fuck," Zander growled rough, and moved in behind her. She shifted higher, accommodating his long legs as he kneeled behind her on one knee, the other foot planted on the floor.

"Let's get you ready." He fondled her pussy.

Bridget shook with need. "Any more ready and I'll be done before you even get inside me."

He chuckled. "I want you to come while I'm inside that tight little pussy."

She shook her backside and peered at him over her shoulder. "Then fuck me. Now."

"Such a greedy lover you are," he groused, a grin on his face.

"All for you," Bridget confessed, heart warm and full.

Playing with her clit, his fingers spread the wetness from side to side. She purred, rubbing her nipples on the lounger.

"I love how responsive you are. Makes me so hard."

She rubbed herself on the furniture harder, shifting her hips in time with his fingers on her nub. Surely she'd died and gone to heaven tonight. Nothing had ever been so good. Zander had already taken her to the stars and back, and here she was, more than anxious to be ridden there again.

Wanton and hungry for her man's cock, she shifted on her knees, lifting her bottom high. Staring back at him, she grabbed a cheek, spreading herself open. "Take me, Zander. Fill me."

He sighed, pressed a kiss to her lower back, and then grabbed the dildo.

She let out a gasp. The glass was cool on her pussy. He spread the toy around, gathering the juices, and pressing it against her clit. Her neck arched, waves of pleasure spiking through her as he played with her.

"Mmm, so wet. This baby is going to slide right into your hot pussy," Zander boasted, as he pushed the head of the dildo inside her.

She tightened her arms around the end of the chaise, breathing fast, as the width invaded her flesh. Each inch had her exhaling hard, each spiral revved the inferno inside her, rubbing against her walls and her juices flowed.

Swallowing a loud cry, she inhaled and held on tight, anxious to have the glass shaft buried to the hilt inside her. She relaxed her inner muscles. Zander's tongue swirled around the bud of her ass. She nearly jumped out of her skin.

"Relax," he whispered.

Shocked and aroused, she gave herself over to his guidance. Sharp sparks of electricity zinged along her rectum. His moist and hot mouth relaxed the hole, while he pushed the dildo the remainder of the way inside her.

He pumped the toy in and out of her. The stimulating spirals twisting hit every inch of her walls and pounded her g-spot. The explosion of nerves inside her that she wasn't aware of nearly sent her over the edge. But she inhaled hard and fought to concentrate on relaxing, not wanting any of this to be over too soon.

Zander's finger circled her bud. She lifted higher, seeking his touch, surprised at the need and electric current coming from that hole. Her whole body hummed with power and yearning.

"Just one finger," Zander muttered. Before she could ask what he meant, one long digit shoved into the hole, filling her.

"Oh!" she gasped, her flesh tingling. In perfect pace and rhythm, he pushed the dildo and his finger in and out. Consumed and filled, Bridget loved every push and pull. As she adjusted to the pace, she lifted her hips, thrusting low at the right moments as he pushed in.

"Damn, fuck, that's hot, babe. Yeah, ride that dildo," he groaned as his finger plunged in and out of her, making her wetter and more on fire than ever before.

"Zander," she groused against the chaise.

"Ahh, yeah, fuck it. I'm hard as a rock." He withdrew his finger inside her ass, only to invade her again, spreading her wide with what she assumed to be two or three fingers. She pushed back, seeking more, desperate to find release.

"Shit. Your ass is made for fucking, babe. I can't wait to get my dick inside there."

"Do it," she begged. "Please, I'm ready."

His touch at her backside abandoned her, as he continued to fuck the toy inside her. She heard the squirt of the lube, and she countered her hips faster, relishing in eagerness and need. Soon he'd fill her everywhere.

Nerves no longer held her captive, only anticipation to have him inside her in both crevices.

He shifted behind her, pushing the dildo into her as she thrust down. "If the pain's too much I'll stop," he promised.

Slowing her movements, she gazed at him. "Please," she whispered, agony and bliss rioting within her. She never needed anything more. It was heaven and hell wanting him so fast, while disliking the fact that it would be over that much sooner.

Zander inched forward, the head of his shaft piercing her near virginal hole. The girth opened her, spreading the hole to accommodate it. Sharp tacks of pain made her shiver.

He pushed the dildo into her pussy. Her eyes crossed, tormented between the rush of pain and carnality attacking her from all sides. Was it possible for a woman to die from such sweet and splendid bliss?

She didn't have time to contemplate it as Zander pushed further into her ass, his fist pumping the dildo into her channel.

"Almost, babe. So tight," he growled.

Taking in a large gulp of air, Bridget instructed herself to relax even more and breathed through the force of each appendage.

"Oh, yeah," Zander mumbled, as he seated inside deeper. "That's it, babe." The dildo glided in and out of her with ease, her juices lathering it, and her thighs.

Intensity built and the burn for release forged toward her. She wanted to thrust down, take Zander fully and be done with it but it took patience to keep gut-wrenching pain at bay. Focusing on her pussy, she welcomed the thrusts of the rounded spirals brushing her muscles. She surrendered to the delight of being fucked. Never before would she have thought she'd receive so much enjoyment from a glass object like this. Alone, she used her fingers or the small silver bullet on her clit to satisfy herself.

She'd find the nearest adult store tomorrow and purchase more toys, in various colors and sizes.

Zander spread cold lube around her hole, a welcoming diversion from the fire consuming her.

A gasp escaped her as he eased in a bit further. Holding her breath, she stayed immobile and let him push in at his own pace. When she thought she'd die of sheer torture, he pushed past the barrier and hit the base of her rectum.

"Ahh, Christ. Fuck, so tight and hot. You're so snug around my dick."

Bridget moaned. Lord, so excruciating but delicious. The sting of having him so tight inside her was overwhelming but also paradise.

"Easy, babe," he instructed as she attempted to move.

"It's burning," she cried, desperate to make it go away.

"I'll pull out. Just a second."

"No," she cried. "Don't leave. Just move. Please. I want it."

"Oh, thank fuck. Take the dildo, babe."

She clasped the glass tight. He grabbed her waist tight, easing slow out of her ass. Bridget stayed still as he got his rhythm and the burn subsided. In and out, Zander filled her over and over again. Her rectum acquiesced to his presence, the sparks of fire in its wake causing her to shiver.

Her nipples hardened. Rubbing them against the chaise, she purred.

"I love fucking you," Zander groaned, moving faster. "Fuck yourself with that dildo."

She shifted one leg, putting a foot flat on the chaise. Zander yelled behind her as she took him in deeper.

Gripping the dildo tight, she pushed it in, nearly falling off the seat from the sheer satisfaction of it.

"Again, babe. You'll love it. Both holes being fucked. Again."

She followed his instruction, dying from pleasure with each thrust. Once she found his pace, she pushed in as he withdrew. In harmonious precision, she absorbed the riotous rampage filtering through her.

Pain and pleasure. Give and take. Push and pull.

She took everything he had to give her, and then some of her own. Pumping the dildo harder and faster, she hung onto the chaise tight as she milked it – and Zander's dick – with all she had.

The carnal decadence in her pussy and ass was glorious. So much wickedness. She yelped as she buried the dildo in further and further, wanting to make it last.

"I want to fuck you like this every day. Every minute of every fucking day," he hissed between clenched teeth. "So damn good."

Faster and faster her hand moved, and she cantered to match his rhythm. His hands helped her ride faster onto his cock, making it awkward to move the dildo but she didn't care. Even having only the tip of it inside her was thrilling.

She shifted, accommodating both and cried out, "Oh God, oh, I'm coming."

The orgasm zinged along her back, raced over her front, and pushed her over the edge. Her juices squirted out of her, forcing the dildo from her. Her muscles tightened and throbbed. She pushed out with her arms, shoving them against the chaise, going rigid as euphoria swept over her.

In her new position, Zander's hardness rammed into her ass, harsh and commanding, and pushed her even further into the abyss.

"Zander, yes. Oh God, yes, fuck me. More. Harder," she begged, her pussy weeping from another orgasm. Such splendid pleasure.

"You're mine. This ass is mine. Fuck, ahh, Jesus."

Bridget welcomed his weight as his hold tightened and he bowed over her back, his dick jerking inside her as he found his own release. She shook with exhaustion and happiness. Her legs and arms felt numb, her knees sore.

She smiled, relishing in the heavy breathing from the man behind her. He'd shown her in so many ways about true passion. He'd been right…they'd wasted so much time.

But they'd make up for it.

Chapter Five

Zander eased out of her, and reclined against his end of the chaise and hauled her into his lap.

Her body hurt, in such delicious ways she figured she'd be grinning about it for days to come.

"That was amazing," Zander whispered.

She lay against his chest, her head on his shoulder and wrapped in his arms. Happiness filled her. She'd always loved her life but had never known such sweet happiness like this before.

"Yes it was," she brushed his cheek with a kiss. "Thank you for being so wonderful and patient."

His chuckled shook her body. "Hell, patience had nothing to do with it. Besides, your body knew what it really wanted. I just went along for the ride."

She laughed along with him.

Silence surrounded them as she cuddled into his embrace. After a few moments, she squeezed his hand. "What now?"

He tightened his hold on her. "I want to explore this new relationship between us. We've been friends and co-workers for so long. But I know there's more."

"A lot more, I think," she whispered, thrilled to be on the same page with him. "I know with school my hours will be limited, but I'll make time for you. For us." She angled her head to look at him.

His gaze met hers and he nodded. "I'll hold you to that." He brushed his lips across hers.

A shiver quaked through her, which she had already grown accustomed to feeling when he touched her, and made her laugh. "You know if you don't stop kissing me, we'll never make it out of this room anytime soon."

Her stomach grumbled, surprising them both.

"Well, sounds like the decision's been made for me. I must feed you." Zander gave her one last kiss, then eased out from under her.

Bridget grinned and watched him. "If you plan to take advantage of poor little old me again, then you'll have to give me food. I won't be able to handle you otherwise."

Zander laughed, shrugged into his shirt and glanced her way. "Poor little old you, huh? You handle me just fine, by the way. But let's get something to eat – to go – then head to your place or mine."

She stood and gazed around. "I guess I'll be going commando," she said as she lifted the tattered remains of her lace underwear.

He laughed uproariously, cocky but charming.

Shaking her head, she eased into her bra then her skirt. "You'll have to buy me new lingerie if you insist on being all manly and He-Man, you know."

Zander yanked her to him, his mouth claiming hers. Desire swirled in her belly and between her legs. She hoped her powerful reaction to him never ceased. Ever.

His mouth lifted. "I'll buy you as many sexy undies as you want, but I prefer you without them." He smirked and let go of her, then stepped into his jeans.

She shoved her arms into the sleeves of her shirt, pondering him. What a man. So strong, fun and exciting. Early yet in the relationship, but the chemistry between them was so strong and blazing, she couldn't imagine it ending any time soon.

Standing at the door waiting for her, his gaze ran over her, going dark with desire. "Damn, dressed or not, I can't get enough of you." He clasped her around the waist when she drew near. "You know, I think I love you."

Bridget's gaze widened. Music to her ears. Happiness and excitement filled her and her heart beat, fast and furious. Oh yes, this was the man for her. She'd denied herself long enough, but deep inside her heart, she'd always known how much he meant to her.

Grinning, she cupped his chin. "That's good. I like that. A lot," Her smile spread from cheek to cheek. "Now feed me, lover. Then I'll show you exactly how much I love you too."

Hips swaying, Bridget exited their private getaway and relished the knowledge that she'd indeed experienced the splendor of falling in love.

The End

Evernight Publishing

www.evernightpublishing.com

38001824R00096

Made in the USA
Charleston, SC
24 January 2015